The Gipsy's Baby

The Gipsy's Baby

Rosamond Lehmann

ET REMOTISSIMA PROPE

Modern Voices

Modern Voices
Published by Hesperus Press Limited
4 Rickett Street, London sw6 1ru
www.hesperuspress.com

First published in *New Writing* edited by John Lehmann
First published as a collection by William Collins Limited, 1946
First published by Hesperus Press Limited, 2006

Designed and typeset by Fraser Muggeridge studio
Printed in Jordan by the Jordan National Press

isbn: 1-84391-427-1
isbn13: 978-1-84391-427-3

Contents

Foreword

It's been said – not least by Jonathan Coe in his 1996 introduction to the reissue of *The Echoing Grove* – that Rosamond Lehmann's overriding thematic preoccupation throughout her career was with romantic love; that central to all of her novels 'are women wounded, wronged or in some way let down by the men into whose trust they have placed themselves'. If this is arguably true of her novels (to no detriment, it must be said; Coe talks of how, to Lehmann, 'the romantic relationship... is seen as the... litmus test of an individual's standards in all other areas'), then it is certainly inapplicable to her shorter fiction, collected herein in its entirety; these five stories represent the only things written to commission in Lehmann's life, for the journal edited by her brother in the 1940s, *New Writing*. And if they move somewhat away from the focus of her longer work, then to what do they move towards? Well, here you will find wintry illness, dampness, fungus, privation, rural squalor. Here, war looms huge. There are the trappings of the materially privileged milieu in which Lehmann was raised, but a diffuse despair bleeds through. Well-tended lawns are here, and amateur dramatics delivered in clipped speech, and the best china, but there is neat vodka in the tea-cups and grief here is not borne with a stiff upper lip but rather is met with a roaring and a wailing and a snot-clogged rage. There is an echo of Mary Webb in the anti-bucolicism of these stories; terribly sad, their main concern is with the awful vulnerability of people and animals, the appalling fragility of their soft bodies and souls. Dylan Thomas once referred to 'cornucopian Rosamond' (see *The Collected Letters*, ed. Paul Ferris), and it's as good an epithet as any; the manifold nature of the human tragedy is here, but being short pieces, and not novels (much less life-times), they are crystallised and condensed, and with what magical, lapidary language:

The silence swelled with immensities of moral conflict and indictment. She stood, accused, by the bed in the dark, and heard the rhythmical throat of night begin to throb and croon again. Bomb, bomb, bomb, bomb. Burn, burn, burn, burn. Down, down, down, down. Fuller, fuller, fainter, fainter. A strong force of our aircraft passing overhead. Impersonally exulting and lamenting, deadly mild, soothing in its husky reiterated burden as a familiar lullaby. Four years safe beneath this portion of the unimpartial sky, Jane, who had called out on the first night of war: 'Do they make special small bombs for children?' heard it now without listening; feared only the unpropitiated presence of the night wind knocking and writhing in the curtain.

That is amazingly adroit writing. The story from which it is taken, 'Wonderful Holidays', features as a character a Captain Moffat, wounded during the Great War, who unceasingly and poignantly tries to convince himself that the reciprocal love between he and his wife is an antidote to the suicidal urgings that forever pulse 'in his sunless head', a mental state of which Lehmann, not being a warrior, must have known very little, but her skill is a universalising one. In fact, it is tempting to see foreshadowings of the clamour of her later life in this – her experiments with mescalin, her very public affair with Cecil Day-Lewis and its equally high-profile collapse, her peripatetic domestic life, and, above all, the abrupt and shocking death of her daughter Sally at the age of twenty-three far away in Jakarta, which instilled in Lehmann an unshakeable conviction in the continuance of the soul after death and a searching for signs from departed spirits that was to obsess her for the rest of her life. All of this reverberates with the stories herein; see the title story, where the untameability of Jannie the dog – effectively the essential and ongoing wildness of the world – brings the two families together, igniting tragedy and causing 'horror [to] topple above the village'.

Lehmann's autobiographical work, *The Swan in the Evening: Fragments of an Inner Life*, was written at a time when her faith in a consciousness that survives bodily death was finally beginning to still 'this painful business', as, in the book, she called the tumult of her life on this planet. The tales in *The Gipsy's Baby* convey directly little of this stage of Lehmann's emotional and spiritual development, but the seeds of it are everywhere within, not least in the vital scrutiny of the duty and craft of the writer, the essential surrender that she must undergo. 'Writers should stay more patiently at the centre and suffer themselves to be worked upon' she declares in the oddly self-reflexive story 'The Red-haired Miss Daintreys', and that seems to be of a piece with the impression given by these stories of the world's friability, the suggestion that another realm awaits behind this prone-to-crumbling veneer. Take, as an example, this passage from the horrific little story 'A Dream of Winter':

> What an extraordinary day, what an odd meeting and parting. It seemed to her that her passive, dreaming, leisured life was nothing, in the last analysis, but a fluid element for receiving and preserving faint paradoxical images and symbols. They were all she ultimately remembered.
>
> Somewhere in the garden a big branch snapped off and fell crackling down.

The tangible world around us goes on dissolving as in it and on it we construct our inner worlds, those banks of memories and considerations and lessons learned and proffered that go to make up our minds, or spirits, or, some might say, our souls. Trapped within the mere skin, every living thing struggles to escape:

every dark sour-smelling haunt of fern and creeping ivy beneath the laurel-planted walks had its particular myth, its genius or indwelling spirit... I remember what, besides myself, hid in the forests of asparagus... what complex phantom rose up from the aromatic deeps of lavender when I brushed white butterflies in flocks off the mauve bushes.

This is the shared sadness of the world, the common horror of every breathing thing; that completion, or at least some kind of defining evolutionary step, is only possible through physical trauma. Lehmann came to not only accept that but to desire it, in her late-middle and old age; but the younger woman who wrote the stories did so in a state of despair and shock at the easily corruptible nature of life's necessary corporeality (witness, for instance, the profoundly disturbing close to 'A Dream of Winter').

Jonathan Coe saw *The Echoing Grove* as a visionary novel because the unhappiness of its main protagonists 'is in fact the instrument of their transcendence', and much the same could be said of *The Gipsy's Baby*. Incarceration in the prison of flesh and bone is the purgatory we are born into and the escape through physical cessation from which is our rapture, and yet within that collection of dying cells some non-physical and therefore undying impulses remain resolute; Captain Moffat's love for his wife, for instance, which seems to be some part of an acquisitive guarantee against his own impermanence. 'The state of not loving was the state of atrocious exile from the human situation', Lehmann wrote in *The Swan in the Evening*, and I couldn't agree more. The stories you are about to read offer one possible route home.

– *Niall Griffiths, 2006*

The Gipsy's Baby

I

At the bottom of the lane that ran between our garden wall and the old row of brick cottages lived the Wyatt family. Their dwelling stood by itself, with a decayed vegetable patch in front of it, and no grass, and not a flower; and behind it a sinister shed with broken palings, and some old tyres, kettles and tin basins, and a rusty bicycle frame, and a wooden box on wheels; and potato peelings, bones, fish heads, rags and other fragments strewn about. The impression one got as one passed was of mud and yellowing cabbage stalks, and pools of water that never drained away. After a particularly heavy rainfall there was water all round the door and even inside, on the floor of the kitchen. Cursing but undaunted, wearing a battered cloth cap on her head, Mrs. Wyatt drove it out again and again, year after year, with a mop. It was an insanitary cottage with no damp course, mean little windows in rotting frames and discoloured patches on the walls.

Mr. Wyatt was shepherd to Mr. Wilson the farmer, who was, I suppose, a shocking landlord; but this idea only strikes me now. It merely seemed, then, that the wretched cottage with all its litter and pieces of shored-up life suitably enclosed the Wyatt brood, and that one was inseparable from the other. Mrs. Wyatt accepted her circumstances in a favourable spirit, and gave birth each year to another baby Wyatt. She was a small crooked-hipped exhausted slattern with a protruding belly and black rotten stumps of teeth. Her beautiful wild eyes were of a fanatical blue, and when she fixed them on you they seemed to pierce beyond the back of your skull. Her face was worn away to bone and stretched skin, and in the middle of each hollow cheek was a stain of rose, like one live petal left on a dead flower.

Maudie, Horace, Norman, Chrissie Wyatt – these names I remember, and can differentiate the owners clearly. Then came three more who reappear to me only as a composite blur, and their names escape me, except that one must have been Alfie, and I still believe the baby's name was Chudleigh. All but one, they took after Mr. Wyatt, and had flat broad shallow skulls, sparse mousish hair – foetus hair – coming over their foreheads in a nibbled fringe, pale faces with Mongolian cheekbones and all the features laid on thin, wide and flat. Their eyes were wary, dull, yet with a surface glitter. They were very undersized, and they wore strange clothes. Maudie owned an antique brown sealskin jacket with a fitted waist and flaring skirts to it. Horace had a man's sporting jacket of ginger tweed that flapped around his boots. The younger ones could not be said to be dressed, in the accepted sense. They were done up in bits of cloth, baize or blanket; and once I saw the baby in a pink flannel hot-water bottle cover. There was something sharp, gnawing, rodent about them; a scuttling quietness in their movements. Their voices too were extremely quiet, delicate, light; entirely without the choking coarseness of the local drawl.

Chrissie was the different one. She had a mop of curly brown hair with auburn stripes in it, a dark, brilliant skin, hollow cheeks, and large rolling eyes like her mother's, only dark. Her brow was knobby, over-developed, disquieting with its suggestion of precocity, of a fatal excess. She frowned perpetually in a fierce worried way, and her prominent mouth would not shut properly. It made a sharp rather vicious looking circle of red round her tiny white teeth. Some charitable person had given her a frock of black and scarlet plaid that fitted tightly to her miniature form and gave her the enhanced reality, or the unreality, of a portrait of a child. I don't think I ever saw her, except once, in any other garment in the whole space of time – how long was it? – during which our orbit touched the orbit of the Wyatt family. The frock did get more and more exiguous; but Chrissie did not grow much, or fill out at all. Against the dun background of her sister and brothers she was isolated and set off: as if her mother's degenerating flesh and bone had combined with the nondescript clay of her father to produce the rest; but Chrissie had been conceived from that bright splash of living blood in her mother's cheek.

Whereas the others all looked, curiously enough, clean in a superficial way, she was always excessively dirty, and this increased her look of a travel-stained child from a foreign country: a little refugee, we would think now. If one met her in the field path and said: 'Hallo, Chrissie,' one said it with apprehension: might she not spit, screech like a monkey, blaze out a stream of swear-words? She never did, though. She bent rapidly down and started to tear up handfuls of turf. When one passed on, she followed, at a little distance, her eyes rolling fiercely, like a colt's, not focusing.

She was often alone, but the others seemed always in a cluster, moving up and down the lane, or hanging over their broken fence. When we went by we always said 'Hallo,' kindly, and they breathed the word back to us in a soft wheezing chorus. They always had colds on their chests. Then, after a brief distance had been established between us, they were apt to direct a piercing whistle after our dog Jannie, a Dandie Dinmont whose long low trotting form riveted them always into a pin of concentrated attention. Patiently bouncing along, as only Dandie Dinmonts do, his shaggy topknot over his eyes, his heavy pantomime head as if barely supported between invisible shafts, he seemed altogether to ignore this magnetising influence. Seemed, I say: we knew he had another life; that *nostalgie de la boue* drove him at dawn and dusk, himself all grey, a shade, to explore the lowest districts and there regale himself with nauseous garbage. We suspected that the Wyatts' back door furnished him a toothsome hunting ground.

Another trait which we could not ignore, but kept firmly on the outskirts of our relationship with him, was his habit of killing cats. He was death on cats. It was curious, for he was a total failure with rabbits, and if he blundered on one in the course of one of his Walt Disney gallops over the fields, he winced if anything and seemed upset. A great many cats visited our garden up till – not after – the time when Jannie, shaking off puppyhood, was beginning to know his own nature; and once he killed three in a week. He left a specimen corpse in the broccoli bed and our gardener came upon it unexpectedly. It was his own cat, a tortoiseshell. The sight turned him up, he said; he hadn't been able to fancy his dinner. We grew to be nervous of exploring the shrubbery, just in case. My father got bored after paying up several high death claims, and gave orders to the outdoor staff to bury at sight and say nothing. At the same time, to our despair, he steeled himself to purchase a muzzle for Jannie. Tearful and crimson, Jess adjusted it, muttering in his ear that it hurt her more than him. But Jannie went out into the paved garden, and beat with his muzzle on the ground like a thrush cracking a snail shell, and within the hour he had got the better of it and came in again wearing it as it might be some kind of Central European military helmet, rakishly, over one eye. Attempting to conceal from him our laughter, we rolled about on the ground and squealed and bit our fingers. We muzzled him a few more times in a spirit of pure frivolity, to await the intoxicating result; but when that delight lost its freshness, the device was altogether discarded; and he ranged once more in all his wild dignity and freedom.

Now we entered upon a halcyon period. No cat, living or dead, haunted the garden any longer. Innocently Jannie's smoke-blue form wove in and out of the berberis and laurel. We told ourselves it was an adolescent phase outgrown.

One evening the back door bell rang. Shortly afterwards a note was carried through and presented: a grimy note of poorest quality.

It seems strange in retrospect how many of the dramas of our lives opened with the loud ping of the back door bell, and were passed along up to the front through a number of doors and voices of announcement. 'A person at the back door, 'M, wishes to speak to you.' 'What kind of a person, Mossop?' 'I reelly couldn't say, 'M. Mrs. Almond give me the message.'

Ladies and gentlemen to the front door, persons to the back. The former could scarcely engage one's imagination: they and the nature of their visits were easily calculable. But a person at the back door emerged, portentous in anonymity, from that other world that ever beckoned, threatened, grimaced, teeming with shouts and animal yells and whipping tops and hop-scotch, with tradesmen's horses and carts, and the bell of the muffin man and words chalked up on palings, just beyond our garden wall. Now and then someone came through the wall and appeared before us, and occasionally it was by the pressure of some extreme urgency – a fatality, a case for the hospital post haste – so that the sight of one or other of my parents walking from the room in answer to such a summons always caused in us a stirring of the bowels.

It was my father who received this note: my mother was out.

He scanned it in silence, then said:

'Is someone waiting for an answer, Mossop?'

'Yes, sir. I understand a young lad. I couldn't say who it would be.'

'Tell him I'll come along presently and see his mother.'

Then he handed the note to Jess. It said that Mrs. Wyatt presented her compliments and our dog had taken and killed their dear little black cat they'd had for a pet three years. It was a bald statement of fact translated with a world of labour into demented arabesques of scrawl and blot, and signed simply: Mrs. Wyatt.

We looked at Jannie sweetly sleeping in his basket by the hearth, and looked away again, seeing a loved face suddenly estranged; angel's face, fiend's face, unaware of crime. 'It's his nature,' muttered Jess; but the pang rooted in the acceptance of such a truth has rarely come home to me more profoundly. This was the first time I knew the inescapable snare of loving a creature with no sense of decency. He was a criminal. We could not change him. We had to love him, go on patching up his betrayals of us, still kiss his tender cruel fur cheeks.

My father sat and smoked a cigarette, and we sat, our books discarded, and waited for him to finish it. He was aware of our feelings and we trusted him. He was never one to blame or to pass a moral sentence. The principle of his life was a humorous benevolence combined with a philosophical scepticism about humanity; and no doubt that perfect generosity of temperament which led him, all his life, to give away his money to anybody who asked him for it, had enabled him frequently to reflect without bitterness: 'It's his nature.' I think the letters in every kind of handwriting, classy, uneducated, youthfully unformed, shaky with age, baring secrets – some trivial, a few tragic – of folly, ill luck, confidence misplaced, with accompanying expressions of everlasting gratitude and pledges of prompt repayment, laid away without comment in a drawer of his desk and found after his death – I think they would fill a volume. The numerous ones beginning: 'Dear Old Man,' were the ones most conducive to cynical reflection. Not that he would have thought so. He never expected to be paid back, and he never was; and in his will he directed that all debts owing to him were cancelled.

We waited in silence, and finally he got up and said: 'Come along, you two, Jess and Rebecca. Down the lane with us.'

Jannie, seeing what looked like the prospect of a walk, stretched himself and skipped forth from his wicker ark and began to prance. 'Don't let him out,' said my father; and in silence we shut the door on his shining, then anxious, then stricken face. Seeing the light fade totally out of him made us feel that the punishment horribly fitted the crime; but far stronger was the sense of wantonly smiting his innocence. The shame, the blame were ours.

We went down the garden, through the bottom gate. It was a hot June evening, and the lane smelt of privet, of dust and nettles. We walked past the end of the row of stumpy prosperous cottages, each with its tended flowery front plot, and came to where the Wyatts' cottage squatted by itself upon its patch of cracked earth and vegetable refuse. There was a decrepit barren old plum tree just beyond their gate, and beneath it were several little Wyatts, perfectly still: waiting for us. Maudie, the eldest, sat with the bald baby on her knee; another, at the staggering stage and with a faint hatching of down on its skull, was stuffed into a wooden grocery box on wheels. Horace, next in age to Maudie, had this vehicle by one handle, and sat there negligently pushing it back and forth. Chrissie was not there. As we came through the gate, it was as though a wire running through them tautened and vibrated. They watched us advance towards them. My father said benevolently:

'Is your mother in?'

'In the 'ouse,' said Maudie, with a jerk of her head.

We were about to pass on when Horace croaked suddenly:

'Your grey dog got our Fluff.'

My father replied regretfully:

'Ah, dear, yes. We've come to say how very sorry we are.'

'We don't like 'im no more.'

'I can understand that,' said my father. 'He's a very bad dog about cats, yet in other ways he's most gentle and loving. It's strange, isn't it?'

Horace nodded.

'We buried poor Fluff,' he said without emotion.

We went on, and their heads swivelled round after us, watching. My father rapped at the door. The lace curtains covering the front room window twitched sharply. After a pause the door was opened by Mr. Wyatt, in his shirt sleeves, smoking a pipe.

'Good-evening, sir!' His tone was bluff and hearty, and his sly little eyes twinkled up at my father in a normal way. I don't quite know what I had expected – that he would burst into tears perhaps, or pronounce a curse upon us – but a grateful relief softened the pinched edges of my heart, and affection for Mr. Wyatt came over me in a flood.

'Good-evening, Wyatt. My little girls are dreadfully upset about this business,' said my father, in a serious man-to-man way. 'I've brought them along because they wanted to tell your Missis and the youngsters how they felt about it. Was poor Pussy a great pet? Are they much cut up about her?'

And what should Mr. Wyatt do but give a shout of laughter.

'Oh that dog, sir! 'E does give me a laugh – always 'as done. Never seen such a dog – 'e's a proper caution. Never think from the build of 'im 'e'd be so nippy, would you? Jiggered if I know 'ow 'e copped that blessed cat. Thought she could look after 'erself. 'E's given 'er many a chase up the tree when 'e's been around. Caught 'er napping – that's what it was.' He chuckled and pulled at his pipe. 'There she was, laid out stiff round by the shed. Not a mark on 'er. 'E done the job double quick – neat, too. Our Chrissie saw 'im at it. She was a bit upset. Fact is,' he added confidentially, 'they was all a bit upset. It's only natural. They thought a lot of that there cat.'

A figure now suddenly materialised behind his shoulder, and it was Mrs. Wyatt, straightening her dark blue apron, tucking in wisps of hair, sending out emanations of wild welcome. She seemed completely overcome by the sight of us on her doorstep and kept uttering whimpers of delight, her ruined gap-tooth mouth opening and closing at us, her great eyes shedding over us streams of radiant blue light.

'Won't you come in, sir? Arthur, why don't you ask the gentleman in, and the young ladies, bless their hearts. To tell you the honest truth, I wasn't feeling quite the thing, and I slipped upstairs to have a bit of a lay-down.'

Her voice, piercing, resonant, with an occasional wailing note in it, pinioned us where we stood while continuing to urge us within. It occurred to me suddenly that Mrs. Wyatt looked very ill. Her lips were a queer colour – violet – and her cheeks beneath the carnation cheek bones were yellow, cadaverously sunken. She looked mad, driven, loving, exhausted. I stared at her until I felt hypnotised; and to this day her face with that something prophetic stamped upon it which I discerned but did not recognise comes before me in all its waste and triumph.

My father excused us from coming in on the score of its getting on for my bed time; and this threw her into a further paroxysm of enthusiasm. She seemed to dote on me for my early bed time: it was a tribute to our superior way of life.

'To be sure! It would be! Bless 'er! Well! It's ever so good of you, sir, I'm sure to trouble to come down. I said to myself: "Now shall I mention it, or shan't I?" Giving you all such a shock and upset – it didn't seem right. But the children did take on so, I didn't hardly know what to do. I thought: "Mrs. Ellison will understand I did it for the best." How is she? Oh she does so much! I'm sure every one in the village worships her. Oh that dog of yours! – artful! – it isn't the word. I said to my husband I'd never have believed it. Always round at our back door always welcome, the bones and that he's buried, and then to take and kill poor Fluff like that. It seems so cold-blooded if you understand. Many's the plate of scraps he's had off her. I used to pass the remark to my husband, what an appetite! – and then gazing up at you so melting out of his big eyes. Ooh, Chrissie did create! – didn't you lovey? Where's she got to now? She's been tight round my legs ever since.' She turned and yelled over shoulder: 'Chrissie! Chris! Come to Mammie, duck! Dad's buried poor old Fluffie. You won't see her no more.'

These (to us) crude and tactless encouragements seemed to fall upon deaf ears. No Chrissie appeared. My father engaged Mr. Wyatt in low-voiced conversation. I saw some silver slip from his hand into the knobby brown-grained hand of the shepherd; and the latter thanked him with a brisk nod and a brief word.

All at once Chrissie darted from the obscurity of the cottage towards her mother. I caught a glimpse of her grimy burning face before she buried it passionately in Mrs. Wyatt's skirts. Another thing I noticed was that a spasm contracted Mrs. Wyatt's lips and forehead, as if the impact made her wince with pain. She put an arm round Chrissie's head and clasped it to her side.

'There's a silly for you!' she cried with rough love. 'Whatever will these young ladies think? She's shy, that's what it is. Ooh, she did create! Never mind, duckie, it's all over now. Mammie'll get you another kitty. Look now, these lovely little ladies have come to see you.'

'To say we're sorry,' muttered Jess heroically.

'Oh dear, and we know they wouldn't have had it happen for the world.'

But Chrissie remained mute, tense, annihilating herself; all of her repudiating us.

My father touched us on the shoulder, and it was all over, and we could go. I had been nervously fingering the wood of the rickety porch, and had my hand raised, picking at the paint blisters. Suddenly I felt it seized and snatched to Mrs. Wyatt's lips. I heard her cry wildly:

'Look at her little white hand!'

Tingling from head to foot with blushes, I was unable to join in the mutual expressions of cordiality and farewell. We went away down the cinder path and when we came to the group beneath the tree my father stopped.

'You know, we're dreadfully sad,' he said. 'We love cats as much as you do.'

They stared at us, their eyes pin-pointing from a great distance. But Maudie said politely:

'Oh well, it can't be helped. It don't matter.'

'Dad says 'e'll beg a puppy for us when Jet at the farm 'as pups,' said Horace.

'Good,' said my father. 'Remember puppies like a nice bowl of water – *clean* water – handy for whenever they want to wet their whistle. And I'll tell you a thing they *don't* like. They don't like to be tied up all day. In the end it makes them so cross they feel like biting people. Just as I'd feel. Wouldn't you?'

They looked extremely wary now, their faces blank with suspicion and alarm. Not a word came out of them. My father walked round behind them to the back of the tree and examined in a meditative way a hole freshly dug in the ground.

'That's a fine hole somebody's dug.'

'We done it for Fluff,' said Maudie. ''Orace done it. But our Dad took 'er away and put 'er somewhere else. 'E said Alfie and them would go digging 'er up all day.'

My father stirred the earth with his toe:

'I fancied I saw something shine,' he said. 'What can it possibly have been? Come and look, one of you.'

Cautiously Horace got to his feet and came and stood beside him.

'Just here,' said my father.

Something gleamed in the loose dry soil at the bottom of the hole. Suddenly Horace crouched and started scrabbling; then he whisked upright again, his face drawn, mottled a dull pink.

On his palm lay some earth and a half-crown piece. He was trembling all over.

'Well, I'll be blessed!' said my father. 'What an extraordinary piece of luck that you should have dug just there.'

Maudie picked up the baby and came and stood beside her brother. The one in the box clambered out and joined them. Finally Horace said in a toneless whisper:

''Oo do it belong to?'

'Why, to the lot of you,' said my father. 'Finding's keeping, you know, when it's buried treasure.'

We went out of the gate, and when I looked back I saw Horace scuttling towards the cottage, his head down, and the little one scuttling after him. Only Maudie remained under the plum tree, her stomach stuck out to support the weight of the child in her arms, staring after us.

'You did drop it in, didn't you, Daddy?' said Jess, who liked to have everything shipshape, with no excuse for mystification.

'I saw you,' I said; and I had; and was in consequence brooding beneath the cloud of too much light. For it had come home to me in a flash, as the coin left his pocket for the earth, that my reading of *The Treasure Seekers*[1] had been at fault, and that my father and Albert Next Door's Uncle had practised an identical deception. This was an absolutely new idea to me, and caused me a shock of disillusionment.

My father sighed and smiled.

Surreptitiously, for fear of Jess's eye, I squinted sideways at my little white hand.

2

That was the first act in our relationship with the Wyatts: unpropitious, fraught with omens. It was my younger sister Sylvia who subsequently insinuated them, first into the garden, then into the house; and so forever into memory and imagination.

Sylvia had long ago swept away any class barriers which she considered irksome, and for preference selected comrades from among the back lane children. In the self-created rôle of Lone Scout, wearing a personally designed uniform girt with a stiff leather belt and stuck with knives, ropes, whistles, assuming a gruff husky voice and a sort of backwoodsman's accent, she roamed the lane and mingled in the seasonal hopscotch and top-whipping. She knew every single one of the children, name, age, details of private life and all. Her experiences must have been interesting – much more so, factually speaking, than my own. I feared the caterwauling noises that floated up in the evenings to the nursery window; I shrank from the drawings and inscriptions upon the pillars of the railway arch. They printed themselves with scorching precision upon the cavern walls behind my eyes, but I passed them furtively, hoping they would – wouldn't – would be rubbed out; as they sometimes were – only to reappear again – by some anonymous purifier working secretly with an indiarubber in the night.

I never thought of the back lane kids as children like myself: they were another species of creature, and, yes, a lower. I imagined their bodily functions must in some nameless way differ from my own. But for Sylvia they were objects of whole-hearted fascination, beings to be emulated and admired. Such posted announcements as: *Rosie Gann goes with Reggie Hiscock*, with accompanying symbols, were transcripts of mysteries into which she had initiated herself without dismay or shame. There never was a little girl less likely to see something nasty in the wood shed. What she did see she accepted with an unwavering speculative eye – an eye that from birth had met the shocks of life impenetrably with one cold answer: 'Just as I expected.' I was fluid, alternately floored and ecstatic; but she was what

I believe theosophists call an old soul, and the parents, nurses, governesses, schoolmistresses of the world impressed on her nothing except a tacit determination to resist their precepts. Jess cried out fiercely: 'Unfair! Unjust!'; and I wept, and hastened to be accommodating, because of a wish to be loved by everybody; but Sylvia gave away no clue that might have provided an opportunity for character-moulding. She learned a number of interesting words and rhymes in the back lane; and sometimes she came in from play with a faintly stupefied expression, as if there had been a good deal to take in.

She used to conduct parties into the garden by the bottom gate, and lurk with them among the shrubbery. My parents were democratic in their ideas, but I doubt if they would have encouraged their visitors, had they been aware of their presence. So far as I know, they never were precisely aware of it. The shrubbery was profuse, in the late Victorian style, containing many a secret chamber and named vantage point. The game was to see unseen. Generally all was silence, but now and then owl hoots, unseasonable cuckoo calls issued from the depths of the foliage: ritual cries, maybe, or merely a leg-pull for the gardeners. But gardeners are, I think, particularly unsusceptible to leg-pulls based on natural phenomena; or perhaps it is that custom has dulled their response to the calls of birds: anyway they gave no outward sign of attention or perplexity.

There were also occasional raids on the cherry, plum and apple orchards during the ripe seasons – triumphs of strategy one and all; differently organised indeed from the wretched affair of the ungentlemanly Barstow boys and the peaches, to which I lent myself: but that is another story.

These were the days when each portion of the garden, every shrub-girdled bay of grass and rose bushes, every dark sour-smelling haunt of fern and creeping ivy beneath the laurel-planted walks had its particular myth, its genius or indwelling spirit. Now, when I go back home, I am confused sometimes by double vision. A veil clouds my eyes, and at the same time a veil is stripped off; for a moment time's boomerang splits me clean in two, and presences evanescent and clinging as webs, or the breath of flowers on the wind, drift in the familiar places, exhaling as they pass a last tingling echo of primeval rapture. Almost I remember what, besides myself, hid in the forests of asparagus; what whispered in the bamboos round the pond, and had power over the goldfish and the water lilies; what complex phantom rose up from the aromatic deeps of lavender when I brushed white butterflies in flocks off the mauve bushes.

Sylvia's myths, intense as mine, were different in their nature, and we never exchanged or shared them. Mine leaned to prettiness and fairies; hers, I feel sure, were bonier, more unromantic, masculine. We ranged ourselves roughly as it were – *Little Folks* against the *B.O.P.* Jess took in *The Children's Encyclopaedia*, and she cleaned out the rabbit hutches and nursed the puppies through distemper, and knitted scarves and mittens – proper, wearable ones – for my father and my brother, while daemonically we roamed in the sacred wood with bloomers torn, and black powder off branches in our matted hair.

Sylvia's customary visitors never came near the house, let alone into it; but the Wyatts did come. They worked away noiselessly, like termites, and in the end our foundations collapsed, and they were in the nursery. It was the summer my mother went back to New England to see her people, and took Jess with her. Our infant brother was sent to the seaside with Nurse, our unpopular Belgian governess returned to her native country for a lovely long holiday, and Sylvia and I remained at home to keep our father company, with only Isabel the nursemaid to supervise us.

It was a beautiful time. All over the household a slackening of moral fibre took place. Mrs. Almond our cook had friends in most afternoons, and we showed off to them and made them clap their hands over their mouths to gasp and giggle and exclaim that we were cough-drops, cures or cautions. Mossop imported a fascinating curly-haired nephew called Charlie, a professional soldier, who played the concertina and encouraged us to sit on his lap. I stayed up to dinner every night. The Wyatts advanced their operations.

One day Sylvia said in an off-hand way:

'Isabel, the Wyatts are in the garden. They want to come up and see our toys.'

Another time Isabel might have replied that want must be their master, or: 'And so does the sweep's grandmother, I dare say. The very idea! What next?' – but she was in particularly mellow spirits that afternoon and she answered: 'Well, I can't see the harm in that. A cat may look at a king, so I've heard tell;' and she went on pinning together the cut-out front portions of a new blue sateen blouse over her opulent bosom, and humming snatches of *After the ball was over*.

She was a strapping girl with red cheeks and a full blue marble eye. She sang loudly, in operatic style, with maniac tremolos, as she went about her work. She had a bottom drawer, and a bone in her leg, and saw handsome strangers in the tea-leaves, and bade us leave a little for Miss Manners, and threatened to give us what Paddy gave the drum; and was apt to answer our questions obliquely with a tag or a saw. She was without tenderness. Her mind was not on us. A set-back in her private life on her day out, or a telling-off from Nurse occasionally made her sulky, and then she was apt to give us sharp pushes and be rough with the comb; but she had a fund of easy animal good nature, and we liked her very much, and admired her looks as much as she did herself.

Sylvia went away, and came back with three Wyatts behind her: Maudie, Horace, Chrissie. They stood in a block at the nursery door.

I said would they like to look in the toy cupboard; but they made no answer. 'There's the rocking-horse,' said Sylvia; but their eyes darted up and down, over the walls, along the floor, not focusing. A deep flush came up and began to burn in Sylvia's cheeks. Nothing more happened. Then in came Isabel, swinging her hips, looking particularly pleased with herself – I suppose the blouse was turning out a nice fit – and crying amiably: 'Well, here's a lot of smiling faces, and no mistake!'

We giggled, abashed, and the Wyatts looked at her in a stunned way. Then a minute ventriloquist's voice came out of Maudie, remarking politely:

'Hope it's no trouble.'

'Trouble? I've got trouble enough without troubling about you. All my ironing to do. Mind the wind doesn't change on those doleful dials of yours, that's all, or we'll all have something extra to mope about. We don't eat children in this nursery, you know.' She picked Chrissie up in her arms and gave her a little shake; and Chrissie strained back, her wreath of hair slipping forward and hiding her face as she bowed it low, low on to her chest, out of Isabel's sight. 'Curlylocks! Oo, aren't you a thin mite! We'd never get a square meal off you, would we?'

A tiny doll's titter issued from the other two, and at that encouraging symptom Sylvia and I broke out in hearty laughs of relief. A section of Chrissie's eye was visible, frantically rolling. Suddenly she pitched forward in Isabel's grasp, flung both arms round Isabel's neck and hung there convulsively, buried and silent.

'Lor' love a duck!' said Isabel after a second's pause, her voice taking on a startled gentler note. 'You cling on like a little monkey, don't you? Just like a little monkey on a stick.'

She carried Chrissie over to the musical box, wound it up and put on a disc. Out tinkled *After the ball was over* in liquid midget notes. She gave Chrissie a kiss and set her down, saying: 'Be a good girl now, there's a love. You're all right.' Then she gave a nod to Maudie and tweaked Horace's ear and went out.

It was all right then: the paralysis was dissolved. Horace mounted the rocking-horse, dubiously at first, clutching its mane and letting out a sharp panicky 'Hey!' whenever it moved; gradually with increasing bravado. Maudie walked softly about, looking at the rugs, the fireguard, the screen we had plastered with cut-out pictures from magazines and seedsmen's catalogues. She looked at the doll's house, and the doll's cot, but she never so much as put out a finger to touch anything. Playing seemed a concept unknown to her. She threw off polite remarks, such as: 'Ain't it a big room?' and: 'Is that your picture book?' She stood with her sagging, broken-down working woman's stance, and looked long at the coloured print of Madame Vigée Lebrun[2] and her daughter above the mantelpiece. I explained that they were mother and child, and that the lady in the picture had executed the work herself. She said: 'Is it hand-painted, then?' I said dubiously I thought it was a copy but that the original was indeed hand-painted. She said however did she manage then, when she'd got both arms round the kid? I was stumped.

After that she said: 'Where d'you keep your clothes and that, then?' and I conducted her to my bedroom, and opened the cupboard. Our wardrobe was far from extensive, but I felt a mounting possessive complacence as I displayed my frocks. She still seemed apathetic, but at the back of her eyes I could now see a fixed point of glittering light. I was overcome by the desire to present her with a pink cotton frock which I disliked. Though I was nine and she rising thirteen I was fully as tall as she. This wish strove with fear of being scolded should the transaction be discovered, and the resulting conflict held me powerless.

She said: 'Which is your best, then?' and for a climax I took down my dancing-class frock of crimson accordion-pleated silk. She put out her hand to touch it, but did not do so.

'We've got bridesmaids' frocks too, from our cousin's wedding,' I said. 'Apricot satin with pearls embroidered on the belt.'

'Where are they, then?' she said.

'Oh, they're put away,' I said. 'We're not allowed to take them out of their tissue paper.'

Feeling suddenly a peculiar revulsion from clothes, I led her back to the nursery, where Horace was still on the rocking-horse, and Chrissie still crouched by the musical box, with Sylvia putting on *Robin Adair*, *The Bluebells of Scotland* and *After the Ball* for her in unbroken succession.

A noticeable thing was their apprehensiveness about any spontaneous moves. We were accustomed to the uninhibited pounces and rushes of our social equals when they came to tea; but the springs of these children were crushed back and could not leap out.

There came a battering and a whimpering at the door, and who should tear in but Jannie, fresh from some round of local visits. We were embarrassed; but they looked at him without ill-will while he gave himself up to the raptures of reunion. Horace even bent to stroke him, remarking:

'You copped our Fluff, you did.'

''E still comes round our back door,' said Maudie. 'Our Mum says she can't like hold any think against a dumb animal when it's their nature.'

We could think of no suitable reply.

Then Isabel came carolling back, and swung Chrissie up again and set her on her lap, saying cheerfully: 'Well now, let's have a look at you. Found your tongue yet? Eh?'

Chrissie nestled against her shoulder, half-hiding, but relaxed, coy. The others came and stood close beside Isabel, trustful, smiling faintly.

'You're all right, Chris,' said Horace.

'Our Mum says she's a funny girl,' said Maudie. 'She says she don't know where she come from. She's not like the others, she says.'

'She can't 'arf bite when she gets 'er temper up,' said Horace.

'Yes, I bites,' whispered Chrissie, beaming.

I think it was the only thing I ever heard her say.

Isabel burst out laughing.

'Oo, you little sinner!' she cried. 'Don't you know what happens to little girls who bite? They get turned into nasty little dogs, they do. Don't you ever do such a shocking thing ever again.' She tilted Chrissie's chin up and looked at her indulgently. It was plain that the beauty of the creature had caught her fancy. 'Two-pennyworth of bad ha'pence, that's what you are,' she said; and then, goodnaturedly, she swept us all out to the garden and told the Wyatts to mind and run along home at once now.

So we accompanied them to the bottom gate, and bade them good-bye.

The visit had been a success. Yet for the rest of the day I felt depressed. I wished never to have known the Wyatts.

A few days afterwards, Sylvia told me that the Wyatts wished to come to tea.

'Did you ask them?' I said.

'No – they asked themselves.'

'I don't really want them much. Do you?'

'I don't mind. Anyway I've told them they can come.'

'I think Isabel might be cross.'

'I shall ask Dad. If he says yes, she'll have to.'

A stubborn sense of obligation was driving her, I could see. Her feelings about the Wyatts were undoubtedly purer, warmer than mine; but in her too, I think, they were beginning to get muddied. Uneasiness was creeping over both of us. We had got what the Wyatts wanted; sense of guilt deprived us of any concentration of forces such as theirs to oppose to them; Jannie had killed their Fluff. We were at their mercy.

That evening Sylvia said: 'Dad, can I have some children to tea?' – and of course he said: 'Yes, my pet,' and inquired no further. So when next morning at breakfast Sylvia announced: 'Dad says we can have the Wyatts to tea,' some flouncing movements were the only outward signs of revolt that Isabel could permit herself.

'Oh, indeed, by all means, have the whole lot in,' she said sweetly. She rattled the crockery on to the tray, and added what I had been waiting for: '*And* the crossingsweeper's family, do, by all means.' This relieved her feelings, and she added with only normal tartness: 'I suppose you've got round your father again to allow it.'

She went out with the tray, and no doubt told them downstairs that next time she'd speak her mind. She was having a bit of an off-day, unfortunately; but also I suspect that the previous visit had been condemned in the servants' hall. The Wyatts had a very low local reputation.

That afternoon Maudie, Horace, Chrissie came to tea. Their hands and faces showed signs of scrubbing, and they were dressed for the occasion. Maudie wore a strange box-pleated dress of violet alpaca, made originally for a far larger and fuller frame. It lent a saffron tinge to her sallow complexion. Chrissie, in a discoloured scrap of pallid Jap silk, had almost lost her personality.

I had expected them to fall on their food and stuff it down with both fists, after the manner of the ravenous in fiction, but they seemed uninterested in tea. I wondered – so full of surprises are people's home lives – if possibly they were accustomed to daily feasts of cream buns and iced cake, and were utterly disgusted by our simple fare. They chewed without appetite at a slice of bread and butter each, and refused ginger-bread, and clearly gave Isabel the pip by their unnatural abstraction from the board. I could hear the caustic comments she was not expressing. Nothing is so likely to produce hatred and contempt in a hostess as distaste manifested at table by her visitors; and when the latter are a trio of despicable, scrubby, under-nourished little brats, the feeling must be deeply intensified. I suppose one factor was that they were so unaccustomed to the ordinary diet of childhood or indeed to regular meals of any sort that they had become more or less indifferent to food. I have often noticed how much less greedy children of the proletariat are than others. One would imagine that they would be more absorbed in the problem of stoking up than the pampered young of the middle and upper classes; but it is not so. They are spare and delicate of appetite, extremely cautious of experimenting, and seem not to wish to stuff themselves even when there is a real opportunity for a blow-out. But when I look back, I see that as regards this particular tea-party it was excess of emotion that deprived the Wyatts of all appetite. At last they had compassed their objective: they had come to tea.

Everybody was quite silent. This time Isabel did not help. It was a relief when the meal was over. Chrissie scuttled to the musical box, Horace to the rocking-horse. Maudie lingered about, looking apathetically at various objects. As soon as Isabel had gone out with the tray, she said to me in her dull voice:

'Where does your mother keep her dresses and that, then?'

My heart sank.

'Oh, some in her room, some in the cupboard in the passage.'

'Let's have a look at them, then.'

Feeling dishonoured and sensing doom, I led the way to my mother's bedroom. I came to the door which since her departure I had not found courage to open; and desolation swamped me as I turned the handle. There was the shrine, empty, its fresh chintzes as if frozen beneath a film of thin green ice, the bed shrouded, the gleaming furniture, the cut-glass bottles, the photographs, the pastel drawing of three little girls in white frocks and blue sashes – ourselves – speaking at me with cold, mourning, minatory voices. All her possessions had become taboo. This was desecration. I loathed Maudie.

'Ain't she got any velvets, then?' said the relentless voice.

'She's taken all her best frocks to America,' I said. 'I think everything's locked, anyway. We'd better go back to the nursery.'

'Go on. Try.'

Fearing she was about to lay hands upon the cupboard, I sprang towards it, and at my touch the carved olive wood door yawned open with a soft complaint, and revealed the long attenuated draperies of various garments hanging down.

'That's her black velvet tea gown,' I said, touching it hurriedly.

'What's that?' said Maudie, pointing.

'That's an evening dress. It's got silver water lilies on.'

'Let's see it, then.'

I took down the green and silver brocade on its hanger, and laid it out on the couch.

'Ain't that 'er best, then?'

'It's one of her best, but she didn't take it because sea journeys tarnish silvery things.'

For a few moments, pride of showmanship overcame my nausea. If I had to go through with it, at least I could tell myself I had done Maudie proud. The dress flowed along the couch, a glittering delight. It was my particular favourite, appearing in my imagination as a sort of transformation scene – a magic pool, a fairy ring in an enchanted wood. I glanced at Maudie, and saw in her eye the same gloating point heightened now to an inexpressible degree. It was the look of someone in a trance-like state of obsession.

It was at this moment that Isabel swept in upon us. The rest is lost in horror and humiliation. We were driven back to the nursery, and the Wyatts were told it was high time to get along home. Off they bundled, noiseless, wary, unresisting. Through a mist, I saw Chrissie in the doorway break from formation, dart back to the musical box, make as if to pick it up, snatch her hands off it, dart back, dumb, to Maudie's side again. Afterwards I was enveloped in a whirlwind of scolding. Explanation was fruitless; I did not attempt it.

That night in bed I wept myself to a pulp and knew that my mother would die in America and that it would be entirely my fault; and nobody came magically to comfort me.

Isabel was particularly nice to us after that episode. I suppose she felt some responsibility with us for the catastrophe; I heard her say to the kitchen maid that those dratted Wyatt kids were on her mind. 'And another any day now,' said Alice; and then they whispered together. She gave us little treats, and encouraged us to have a picnic party of friends of our own class, and helped to make it go with a bang. Then, perhaps to demonstrate the difference between riff-raff like the Wyatts and well brought up inferiors, she asked little Ivy Tulloch to tea with us.

Ivy was the only child of the head gardener at Lady Bigham-Onslow's, impressive neighbour, and Mrs. Tulloch and Isabel were dearest friends. Isabel had tried before to offer us little Ivy, but we had always vigorously rejected her. This time we felt our position shaky, and dared not protest.

She was a fat bland child with bulbous cheeks and forehead, and we despised her prim smug booted legs and her pigtails bound with glossy bows. She had far more and smarter frocks than we, and insertion and lace frills to the legs of all her knickers; whereas we had only one ornamental pair apiece, for parties. She was kept carefully from low companions, never played in the lane, and was made ever such a fuss of by Her Ladyship.

The arrangement made without consulting us was that she should trot along about four o'clock for a nice game with us, and that her Mummy should pop in after tea to have a chat with Isabel before taking her home.

Four o'clock came and went: no Ivy. We began to feel hopeful: she had forgotten the day, perhaps, or been struck down by measles. At five we ate the doughnuts bought to tempt her dainty appetite. By five-thirty we had totally erased her distasteful image from our minds, and were agreeably immersed in our own pastimes. Then we heard the back door bell ring sharply: and Isabel, exclaiming: 'There!' went rustling down at top speed. Shortly afterwards, two pairs of footsteps returned, two voices sounded in the passage, engaged in emphatic thrust and counterthrust. We recognised the refined and breathy tones of Mrs. Tulloch, and the punctuating gasps and exclamations of Isabel. They went into the night nursery, hissed together for a little longer, then flung open the dividing door and descended upon us.

A flaming spot stood in either cheek of Mrs. Tulloch, and there was a look about her, we saw it at a glance, of the mother fowl defending its young. She kept saying: 'Don't give it another thought, Isabel, I beg. I wouldn't want to cause any trouble, not when it's children'; and Isabel kept repeating that she never would have credited it, never, the wickedness.

Chaotically, the facts emerged. Stunned, we pieced them together. They were these. Little Ivy, dressed in her best and feeling a wee bit shy, bless her, but innocently trusting to be met as arranged by Isabel at the back door, had come tripping across the fields at the appointed time. But at the turn of the lane, who should be lurking in wait, pressed up against a small wooden side door in our garden wall – who but Chrissie? And then what happened? Chrissie Wyatt had had the downright demon wickedness to declare to Ivy she wasn't wanted inside, that she, Chrissie, had been specially posted there by us to tell her so; that it was horrible, awful in there anyway, a kind of torture chamber; nobody was allowed to talk, *not even to smile* at the tea-table; and Ivy had best run along home quick before anybody appeared to beckon her within. So what was left for Ivy but to hurry back home to her Mummy, frightened out of her little wits, sobbing her little heart out?

'Wait till I catch her!' muttered Isabel. 'I'll give her not even smile at tea. When I think!... Cuddling up to me so loving and... The spitefulness! It only shows... And I hope it'll be a lesson. If I hadn't got your word for it, Doll, I'd never have credited it, never. Who'd ever fancy a 'uman child could have the artfulness, the wicked artfulness – a scrap of a thing like her. The downright impudence! Makes you think she can't be right in her head...'

'The devil's in her, if you ask me,' said Mrs. Tulloch; adding sweetly: 'You said they came to tea last week, did you, dear?'

'It wasn't my doing,' said Isabel. 'They got round their father, as per usual.'

'Ah well! We all know a certain gentleman's kind heart. But as I always say, it's all very well. Right's right, when all's said and done.'

'Ah, and it's easy to be soft when it's others have the trouble. That's where it is.'

'And some will always take advantage, that's one thing certain.'

Together they went on intoning judgment and sentence on Chrissie.

'Makes you wonder where she'll finish up.'

'Mark my words, if she goes on like this, she'll come to a bad end.'

'It's the bringing-up – you can't wonder really.'

'Bringing-up it may be, but I always say when a nature's bad, bad it is. You can't alter it. Be your station high or low. Many's the time I've passed the remark to Tulloch.'

Meanwhile we were dumb, aghast. Had we been told that Chrissie had laid a charge of dynamite at our gate and blown up Ivy, the shock could not have been greater. We had to agree, it only showed, we must let it be a lesson. Yet we could not regret the catastrophe to Ivy, or feel drawn towards the injured parent, in whose strokes at the Wyatts we apprehended a back-hander at ourselves; and whom in any case we were debarred from liking owing to her squint and her manner – genteel, patronising, obsequious.

'Now take my advice, dear, and put your foot down another time. If you'll excuse me mentioning it, right's right, and it's best to start as you mean to go on. I dare say it's not my place, but they hadn't ever ought to have set foot, dear, and you know it – though far be it from me to blame you. Still – they're not exactly a clean lot, are they? You wouldn't want yours to pick up anything, would you? – not with their mother away.'

With that she rose and adjusted her hat and said she mustn't stop. She'd only popped along because she knew we'd be worried.

'I left the poor mite sitting on her Daddy's knee, but she'll be fretting for me if I don't get back. Oh, Tulloch, he was upset! You know what men are – he thinks the world of her, it's only natural. I don't know what he didn't want to do. But I said, now we don't want to make trouble, not when it's children. And don't go worrying Her Ladyship with it, I said. Her Ladyship takes ever such an interest in Ivy, you know, always has done since she was a mite in a pram. I said, you'll only upset her – there's no need to go worrying her.'

'Well, I'm sure I hope,' said Isabel, with a stony glance at us, 'you'll find it in you to let her come another day instead.

I'm sure the girls are as upset as me to think it should have occurred.'

'Thanks, dear,' said Mrs. Tulloch, with a sort of repudiating graciousness. 'Perhaps later on when she's over the shock. She's such a sensitive wee soul – you never know what a shock like that will do to a sensitive child. Bless her, she'd got herself quite worked up. "Oo, Mummy," she said to me when I was changing her, "will they have rosebuds on their frocks like me?" The things children think of! "Shall I take my new dolly?" she said. "Will they have some big dollies there? – bigger than mine?"' She uttered a tender deprecating laugh, and cast a glance round our doll-less nursery. 'Well, ta ta, dear. Now don't brood about it, I do beg.'

'I've a good mind,' said Isabel, 'to go down this very minute and speak my mind to her mother.'

'Now, dear, take my advice and don't do no such thing. You never know what sort of answer you'll get from that sort of person. She might turn reelly rude, and then you'd regret you ever gave her the opening.'

'You may be right,' said Isabel. 'Still—'

Still – later on that evening, after we were in bed, Isabel stood by our bedroom window, fingering the curtain, looking out over the garden, arrested in an unfamiliar pose, a quietness that suggested brooding, almost dejection. From this window, the chimney of the Wyatts' cottage was just visible between the poplars. Flat on our pillows, we watched her. Suddenly we heard her say quietly: 'It was jealousy.' She was speaking to herself. Then: 'Poor little beggar.' She heaved a deep sigh, shook her head. 'Ah well, what you can't cure, you'd best let alone.'

She bade us good-night with customary briskness, and went away.

Next morning, I wanted to go to the creek to hunt for some particular water plant for my collection of pressed wild flowers. Short of making a long and dreary detour through the village, it meant passing the Wyatts' cottage; and the idea of running into a group of them was painfully embarrassing. But Sylvia lent me moral courage, and, declaring that since we obviously could not avoid the lane for the rest of our lives it was best to bare our bosoms at once for the encounter, offered to accompany me. We went together down the lane, and the way was clear. The cottage looked deserted. But when we came back about lunch time they were all there, every one of them, in a huddle by their gate. The next to youngest sat in his soap box, the baby lolled its head on Maudie's shoulder. There was no movement among them except the slight turn of their heads as they watched us approach.

'Hallo,' we said sheepishly, not looking at any particular one of them.

''Allow.'

As we passed, Horace croaked suddenly:

'Our mum's gorn to the 'ospital. She's bad. The amb'lance come for her.'

'Last night,' said Norman, 'our dad 'ad to go for the doctor. Then the amb'lance come.'

''Er 'ead was bad,' said Alfie.

One of the younger ones piped:

'Make it better at the 'ospital. Then she come back.'

'Our dad's gone on 'is bike to see 'er,' said Horace.

We said we hoped she would be better soon. We could feel the after-quivers of catastrophe reverberating through the group, but we could not think of anything else to say. Maudie had not spoken a word. Awkward, wishing to make a friendly gesture, I approached her. I had a weakness for holding babies, and though I could not feel drawn to this one, still it was a baby; and I asked her timidly if she thought it would come to me.

''E's all right,' she said indifferently, scarcely glancing at me. Impossible to believe that this was the same Maudie whose stoat-like concentration had so weighed upon me. Then I heard her mutter, in the voice of a sleep-walker: 'We got enough babies, anyway.'

Then, as if accosting a stranger to ask the way, she looked at me with a faint contraction between the eyes and said ungraciously:

'Where is the 'ospital, then?'

I did not know.

'It's a good way off,' she said. 'That I do know.' She shifted the baby a bit and relapsed into indifference. Chrissie was hiding behind her, and involuntarily I caught a glimpse of her face. It was pinched, sallow, drab, and she was almost indistinguishable from the others.

We hurried home to tell Isabel, and found that news of the calamity had already reached her. She shut us up when we attempted to question her, but asked us rather sharply if they'd said whether they'd had their dinners. We had not thought of this. For us, meals were things that appeared automatically on the table at punctual intervals, were eaten, removed again. She appeared absent all through lunch, bit her finger, and after she had cleared away, came to us and said:

'Now be good girls and sit down with your books a bit, like your mother wished you to do. I'm just going to pop down and see if those young Wyatts are all right.'

Feeling a warm rush of affection for Isabel, we obeyed her. She came back not long after, still laconic, and merely said they were all right, various neighbours had taken them in and given them their dinners. They were playing now in the lane, along with some others, and seemed quite bright.

The kitchen maid ran upstairs with a belated post-prandial cup of tea for her, and they retired together to the nursery pantry while she drank it. Terrific whispers came forth, and my ears, ever agog, caught such words as 'raving' and 'water on the brain' as I lingered past them on my way to the bathroom.

I told my father that evening when he got back from London, where he went four days a week to edit a literary journal; and immediately he took his hat and walking-stick and went down the garden to see Mr. Wyatt. He was away some time, and when he came back, his face looked sorry. He told us that poor Mr. Wyatt was very worried. Mrs. Wyatt was dreadfully ill. After all his long bicycle ride, they had not allowed him to see her: she was too ill. She had had a baby, and the baby had died. I knew, and did not know, and could not ask about the unmentionable connection between this and her mortal sickness.

Then he rang the bell and told Mossop to telephone to the hospital first thing in the morning, and inquire for Mrs. Wyatt, and get the message sent down to Mr. Wyatt. Then he went over to the garage and told Gresham, our chauffeur, to hold himself ready to drive Mr. Wyatt to the hospital at any moment of the day or night.

We felt comforted, almost elated. Our father had the situation in hand, and everything would probably be all right.

It was the next night after supper. Sylvia had gone to bed, and I had been allowed an extra half-hour for *David Copperfield*. My father and I sat reading in the library. It must have been nearly nine o'clock. There had been a heavy thunderstorm earlier in the evening, and the sky, instead of clearing in the west with sunset, had remained dun, murky, overcast; and we had drawn the curtains to shut out the lugubrious dusk. All of a sudden came a sound of running on the gravel path outside. Then a frantic drumming on the French windows. My father went white as paper, as he always did at any sudden shock. Again. Again. Paralysed with terror, I watched him walk across the room, draw back the curtains, press down the handle. The doors fell back and there on the step stood Mr. Wyatt, hatless, haggard, wild.

'Wyatt, my dear chap, come in, come in,' said my father, all haste and gentleness, taking his arm and drawing him across the threshold. They stood together in the bay of the window, silent, their heads bowed down; one so tall, dignified, white-haired, the other so small, brown, and gnarled, his poor coat hanging off him, his hair plastered in dark dishevelled strips over his bald head. He drew great labouring breaths as if he had been running for miles, and I saw that his clothes were soaked with rain and sweat. His throat and lips kept moving and contracting, but no sound came. My father stole an arm around his shoulders. At that he cried out suddenly in a terrible threatening voice, like an Old Testament prophet:

'She's gone, sir!'

My father nodded. I heard him murmur: 'Rebecca, run along,' but I was too petrified to make a quick move, and next moment the storm was loosed. Mr. Wyatt began to walk up and down, up and down. The appalling dry sobs torn out of his chest seemed to fling him about the room. He passed my chair with glaring eyes fastened upon me, and took no notice of me. An overpowering smell emanated from him – his clothes, his body, his agony – and his terrible voice went on racking him, bursting and crying out.

'She's gone, sir! They never let me see 'er – not once since they took 'er away. Not till the end. Better not, they said, she won't know you, Mr. Wyatt – she was raving, that was it. They sent word down at dinner-time – come at once. Thanks to your kindness, sir, I got there quick. 'E was good, your shuvver – 'e give me a packet of fags and 'e never stopped for nothink. She's going, they said... It's all for the best, Mr. Wyatt... It was 'er brain went – brain fever or that – some word or other – I never did understand sickness. Why should a thing like that fly all over 'er like, in a couple o' days? She was always strong and 'ealthy, wasn't she? She never complained – only to say she was fagged like these last few months – and a bit of a backache. I thought that 'ud right itself when 'er time come. I thought – I never thought... She never... She 'ad the best of attention, didn't she, sir? Do you think they give 'er proper attention there?'

'My poor Wyatt, I feel convinced they did,' said my father.

'I never saw no doctor. They don't always trouble so much about poor people and that's a fact, sir. She's going, Mr. Wyatt, the nurse said... She was a pleasant spoken woman. She won't know you, she said. They'd got 'er in a room separate... She died private anyway – not in a ward along of... She didn't fancy the thoughts of that... She never wanted to go to the 'ospital. "Don't let them take me, Jim," she says that night – just before she come on so queer. "I'll never come out alive." "Don't talk so foolish, girl," I says. "You'll be back along of us all next week." What could I do, sir? I 'ad to let 'er go, didn't I? I 'ad to abide by what the doctor said?'

'Of course, of course. It was the only thing to do, Wyatt. It was a hundred to one chance, you know. We knew that.'

'A 'undred to one chance – Ah!... She was peaceful when they took me in. She died peaceful anyway. She 'ad 'er 'ands laid out on the sheet – 'er eyes shut... "Now, my girl," I says... Oh, but 'adn't she fallen away in the short time! It would 'ave 'urt you to see 'er. It 'urt me crool. "Now my girl," I says. "We want you back 'ome, don't we? The little 'uns is fretting for you." I thought that might rouse 'er... She never stirred nor took no notice... I sits there beside 'er, on and on. Then I leans over to 'ave another look at 'er. All on a sudden 'er eyes flies open as wide as... She stares right up at me... She knew me at the last, that I do know. That nurse comes in again then... "She's gone," she says. "Poor dear,"... and covers 'er face over... Sir, do you know what they says to me? She didn't never ought to 'ave 'ad another, they says. It was 'er time of life. She was too wore out, they says. She'd 'ad too many. I...' He struck his forehead with his clenched fist. 'God knows we 'ad enough mouths to feed.' His voice broke, trailed off; hopelessly he shook his head. Then he cried out: 'I loved my wife, sir! They can say what they like – nobody can say different. We was happy... A happy family... She thought the world of them – the 'ole blessed lot. "I wouldn't be without one o' them," she'd say...'

He fell silent, but went on walking up and down. My father took the opportunity to come over to me and whisper that I was to go to bed – he would come presently and see me. He gave me a kiss. Doubtful whether or not it would be correct to say good-night to Mr. Wyatt, I hazarded it finally in a tiny voice, scarcely expecting any response. But he answered with dignity:

'Good-night, missy, God bless you. I must ask your pardon, sir, for coming like this upsetting you and little missy here. I 'ad ought to 'ave thought. I thank you for all your kindness. You've been a friend, sir. Yes, a friend. I must get along 'ome to the young 'uns. Got to think of them now, haven't I? Got to break it to them. Maudie, she's a good girl, but...' He shook his head with the same hopeless perplexity, and adding: 'Good-night, sir, God bless you,' made for the window.

'Wyatt, my poor fellow, don't dream of going like that,' said my father tenderly. 'Sit down and rest yourself and take a drop of brandy with me. You're thoroughly exhausted. Here.'

He pulled forward an armchair and Mr. Wyatt sank immediately into it without another word, his elbows on his knees and his head in his hands. The decanters were on the table and my father was pouring out brandy in liberal measure as I slipped out of the room.

I told Isabel what had happened, and she was kind to me and brought me hot milk to stop my shivering after she had helped me to bed. Great tears dripped down her face, and she blew her nose loudly and muttered if only there was something she could do.

A little later I heard voices in the garden and crept to my window to look out. The moon was up now, softly breaking the clouds, and I saw Mr. Wyatt and my father walking together across the misty lawn towards the lower gate. Their voices rose and fell. Mr. Wyatt was quiet now. The prophetic howl had gone out of his throat, and his guttural voice, his voice that seemed almost choked with soil, twined with thick roots, with tubers, sounded much as usual; and my father's voice, which was both light and rich, answered him musically.

Still later on, he came up and sat on my bed and told me how very sorry he was I had had to witness so painful a scene. He explained and comforted as best he could, and made me feel better. I could bear to accept the fact that that was how human beings behaved in the first anguish and indignation of bereavement. What I could not bear, then, was to see him wipe away the tears that kept rolling down his face.

I lay awake and imagined all the children huddled crying and wailing in the cottage. I saw Maudie's face; I tried to imagine Chrissie's; and I saw Mrs. Wyatt stretched dead, her hands folded, in the hospital bed, taking absolutely no notice of them all. I thought the two stains of colour must still lie in her snow cheeks, like roses in December.

After that, the sinister pattern broke. We went away to join our infant brother and nurse at the seaside; and plunged in the happy trance of waves, rocks, sand, we let slip the Wyatts from our minds. My father joined us for a week, brought us all home, and then went to Liverpool to meet my mother and Jess.

We painted WELCOME HOME in white letters on a strip of scarlet bunting, and were busy attaching it to the gateposts of the drive, when we saw Horace, Norman, Alfie and the soap-box one standing under the wall, watching us.

'Hallo,' we said.

''Allow.'

We looked at them furtively and they seemed much as usual except that the three younger ones had new suits on. They watched us with their usual mixed look, incurious yet attentive, as we sat each astride a brick post and lashed rope round the stone ball on the top to hold our banner in position. I felt suddenly that we were doing something silly; and directly I had said: 'Our mother's coming back from America this evening,' I blushed deeply, realising the tactlessness of mentioning the return of a mother.

'It's nice,' stated Norman, in a flat way.

We called directions to each other, and they went on watching, and by and by we got down and surveyed our work. It was a bit crooked but it flared out with loud brilliance upon the shining blue September air. In another hour our parents and Jess would drive in under it. We could not help wondering if Jess would whole-heartedly approve of such a blatant display of feeling.

Horace said:

'They're going away to-morrow – the three of 'em.'

'Where are they going?'

'To the Institution.'

Silence. We did not know what he meant.

'Our dad said for us all to stay together and we'd manage, but that lady said it was too much for Maudie, she hadn't ought to do it. She come and see 'er. She said Maudie couldn't give 'em what they needed, so she spoke to our dad.'

'Our dad cried,' said Alfie.

'So she said they'd be better off in the Institution. She wanted for the baby to go too, but Maudie wouldn't let 'im go.'

'Maudie cried,' said Alfie.

'The lady said it was ever so nice there. They was ever so kind to children. They 'ave a Christmas tree and all. So our dad said to 'em to be good boys and learn their lessons and 'e'd 'ave 'em out soon. 'E's going to get a better job and then we'll 'ave a reel 'ousekeeper and it won't come so 'ard on Maudie. 'E bought 'em new suits.'

'And we got sixpence each to buy sweets,' said Norman.

'And a horange,' said Alfie.

'What about Chrissie?' I said.

'Chrissie's going to stop at 'ome. She went and 'id 'erself when the lady come. One of our aunties wrote a letter. She said she'd take Chrissie and bring 'er up just like 'er own. But Chrissie created so our dad said for 'er to stop at 'ome.'

'So there'll only be the four of us at 'ome now,' said Norman.

'Maudie and 'Orace and Chrissie and baby,' said Alfie.

Their voices were important, not pathetic. The family had obviously been the object lately of many a local charitable scheme, both private and official; and this had set them all up in their own estimation. I felt vaguely that a number of well-disposed people were interested, many benefits were being conferred, and everything was turning out as well as could be expected.

It was time to go and tie a festal bow on to Jannie's collar, so we said good-bye, and went away.

But when I asked Isabel what the Institution was and she replied the workhouse, I knew enough about society to know that disgrace had come upon the Wyatts; and though I was sorry and disturbed, I felt once again what a very low family they were, and how they and their house and their misfortunes emanated a kind of miasma which the neighbourhood could neither purify nor disregard: as if a nest of vermin had got lodged under the boards, rampant, strong-smelling, not to be obliterated.

Now and then I saw Chrissie passing to and from school or playing in the lane among a group of contemporaries. She looked as usual, in her plaid frock. She never smiled, or took any notice of me. Mr. Wyatt continued to be seen about the sheep folds, smoking his pipe. My mother went to see him, and then went again and took Maudie some clothes. Maudie told her she was managing nicely. Dad helped her in the evenings when he got home from work. Sometimes he undressed the baby all himself and gave him a wash and put him to bed: he'd never taken so much notice of any of them as he did of this baby. Yes, the baby had a cold on his chest, but she'd rubbed him, and he was ever so bright and eating well.

There was a neighbour, Mrs. Smith the washerwoman, who was kind. Once I ran down with a message from Nurse to ask her to wash the nursery sofa cover in a hurry and Maudie was there, sitting slumped in a kitchen chair, drinking a cup of tea, silent, grimy, greasy, her hair screwed and scraped up into a bun with huge hairpins. She had put it up, I suppose, to mark the fact that she was now a woman: one of a thousand thousand anonymous ones who bear their sex, not at the unconscious, fluid, fructifying centre, as women who are loved bear it and are upborne by it; but as it were extraneously, like a deformity, a hump on their backs, weighing them down, down, towards the sterile stones of the earth.

In October, the gipsies came back. They came twice a year, in spring and autumn, streaming through the village in ragged procession, with two yellow and red caravans; men in cloth caps, with handkerchiefs knotted round their throats, women in black with cross-over shawls and voluminous skirts, some scarecrow children, and several thin-ribbed dogs of the whippet race running on leads tied, much to Jess's disquiet, under the shafts of the caravans.

They were a raffish, mongrel lot, with bitter, cunning, wizened faces and no glint of the flash and dash that one is conditioned to expect. But there was one noble beauty, a middle-aged woman, short, ample of figure, with gold earrings and a plumed black hat, who came regularly to the back door with a basket of clothes' pegs to sell. The eyes in her darkly rich, broad face glowed with a veiled and mystic fire, and her voice came out of her throat with an indescribable croon on one low note. Isabel always went flying down to buy some pegs – it brought bad luck to turn the gipsies from the door – and once I went with her to watch the transaction. Superstition made Isabel excessively polite, not to say conciliatory, quite unlike her usual style of bridling badinage and repartee with the tradespeople.

I smiled at the woman, and at once her face seemed both to melt and to sharpen, and she caught my hand in hers and began to mutter. I felt the hardness and dryness of her strong hand. My eyes sought hers and were immediately lost in the fathomless gaze she bent upon me. I could not look away, and my panicking senses began to swoon beneath the torrent of unintelligible words poured over me. Something in my face, she said – my fate, my future, a long, long journey… something I could not bear to hear. Then suddenly it stopped; and she asked in quite a different, whining voice if there were any old clothes to-day – any shoes – a pair or two of the little lady's cast-off shoes now for the children – a coat, now – an old jacket for her man. I heard her drilling away at the resisting Isabel as I made off upstairs, my heart still thumping loud with terror. After that I was convinced that the gipsies designed to steal me, and ventured to tell Isabel so; and though Isabel told me not to be so soft, all old gipsy women went on like that, I would never, after this incident, go through the gravel pit field where they always camped so long as the caravans were there.

The gravel pit itself was a romantic spot, overgrown with grasses, clover, brambles, wild rose bushes and bryony. In spring it harboured the most exciting birds' nests – once I found a goldfinch's – but in autumn it was particularly enchanting, when one could rove from one slope to another picking blackberries, hips, and branches of the dogwood that flushed the air so rosily on grey days and blue. Also there were fossilised sea-urchins, petrified fragments of shells lurking among the stones and sand of the old quarry-workings. I spent hours of my childhood there, wandering in a voluptuous, collector's daydream, or lying hidden in one of the many secretive hollows.

It was October. From the nursery window I looked out over the familiar view of shrubbery, lawn and apple orchard, and saw between the thinning boughs of the poplars that bordered it a glimpse, a mile or so away, up the hill, of two red and yellow caravans nestling in a corner of the gravel pit field. The beech woods rose up directly behind them, clasping them as in the curve of a tender shoulder. I saw blue smoke rising, figures sitting on the steps, children tumbling in the grass. I could also see a group of local children hanging over a gate, watching them, a little distance away: the scarlet frock of Chrissie was among the group. I remember thinking then what a fascination the bright roving caravans must have for her; how congruous a part she would seem of the life of fairs and gipsies. I felt faintly anxious and depressed, wondering if the woman had yet been to the back door, hoping that next day the corner of the field would be empty of its load of alien humanity. All the reasons I had for melancholy came down to weigh upon me: Jess, who had not been very well, absent for the winter, gone to share bracing air, riding and education with some cousins near Brighton; our unpopular governess back from Belgium in a day or so, and myself left to bear the brunt of her without Jess. Then I remembered Mrs. Wyatt whom I sought to forget, and how she also had seized my hand; and felt I was singled out in a disquieting if gratifying way by this coincidence: wild forces both, and I, so passive, their inexplicable point of explosion.

What happened next is hard to put down in any exact way, because so much was concealed from us, we had so much to conceal, that sometimes I think I dreamed it all. Suddenly one day out broke the melodrama; but at once we were hurried away from it, and its development reached us only as it were in snatches, in disjointed echoes from the wings or by the furtive peeps we contrived through the lowered curtain. Horror toppled above the village for a short while, then sank back and vanished; and everybody drew a great breath and burst out in chattering, exclaiming, head-shaking; and all the children who had been snapped indoors after school by wrought-up parents were let out to play again; and everything was as before, except for the usual scatter of flotsam left by the retreating tide; and except for one small figure carried away on it, vivid but dwindling.

The gipsies went away. Two or three days later, a peculiar vibration began in the village. It was confined at first to the children. In the afternoon, we were messing about in the laurels by the garden gate, when two of Sylvia's associates, sisters called Cissie and May Perkins, came past and beckoned portentously to us. They said:

'Can you keep a secret?'

We said yes. They said:

'There's a little dead biby in the gravel pit. We ain't allowed to tell 'ow we know, but we do know. Cross your hearts and swear by the Bible you won't tell no one.'

We did so. They said:

'We know because Chrissie told us. She found it. It's under some bramble-bushes. It's got no clothes on. It's a biby boy. She says the gipsies left it there.'

'Do you mean they killed it?' we said.

'Dunno.'

We were silent, beholding the monstrous image of a dead naked baby boy under the bramble bushes. We said:

'Oughtn't somebody to be told?'

'She says on our solemn oath we're not to. We're not to tell our mums nor no one. She says after three days the gipsies may come back and take it away. She's going up to-morrow to see.'

'Why does she think they'll come back for it?'

'Dunno. She says that's what they do. She says if the gipsies knew she'd found it they'd do something downright awful to her.'

'What would they do?'

'Murder 'er and bury 'er.' They added: 'Be down by the gate to-morrer afternoon when we come out of school. We'll tell you if it's still there.'

Next day at the appointed hour they said:

'She's been up to look, and it's still there.'

We were to wait another day, and cross our hearts we'd tell no one.

But that evening some overwrought child broke down and unloaded the news to its parents. All the village began to hum. We were made aware of this by the gathering and whispering of Nurse, Isabel and the others in the servants' hall; and by the fact that our mother called us to her and said with some severity:

'Now girls, I want you to promise – especially you, Sylvia – not to talk to any children in the lane just at present. If they see you in the garden and call out to you just wave politely and go away. There may be a case of measles in the village and I don't want you to run any risk of contact. I don't say it is measles, we must wait a few days to make sure. But you needn't give any reason. Do you understand? Promise now.'

We promised.

That night while Isabel was brushing my hair, she remarked to Nurse.

'Not mentioning any names, someone told me they're under suspicion, that lot, for the same line of thing before; only they never could fasten it on them like. Nice, isn't it?'

Nurse shook her head and uttered a series of sharp tongue clickings. She said:

'Ah, there's more in it than meets the eye.'

'Mark my words,' said Isabel. 'It's that man. You know the one – the older one with the nasty expression of face. I always did think he looked the part.'

'If you ask *me*,' said Nurse, 'they're all in it. The shock for that little mite! – I can't get her off my mind.' After a pause she said: 'Have they got back, did you hear by any chance?'

'Mm,' said Isabel.

Nurse queried with her eyebrows.

'No,' said Isabel. 'It's inky black out. Jim and old Gutteridge had lanterns, but I don't think they fancied the job in the dark, if you ask me.' She giggled. 'I don't blame them neether.'

Nurse told her rather sharply to get on with our hairs, do, and not chatter so.

We understood that an expedition of householders had visited the pit with lanterns, and returned empty-handed.

Next day as I came back at noon from my hour of German with Miss La Touche (cultured spinster and traveller), I saw a sight that froze my blood. It was the local constable emerging from the school-yard, grasping Chrissie by the hand. Her face was down on her chest, her hair over it. With every step she struggled to fling herself back. The constable seemed to be attempting genial encouragement, but he was not built or endowed for soothing. He was the very type of rustic policeman – burly, beefy, flaxen, slow of wits and speech. He was plainly embarrassed by his task and wore a sheepish grin. There was not another child in sight: all kept in. Together, slowly but surely, they turned up the hill towards the gravel pit.

Later on, in the afternoon, another kind of hum began to develop. The silence that had hung over the lane gave place to the customary commotion. The sounds that came out of the servants' hall seemed to contain gasps of staggered somewhat ghoulish incredulity. There seemed also a note of disappointment or disgust – as if there had been a let-down after a promised sensation. I heard Nurse say to Isabel that's what came of letting your nasty imagination run away with you.

'Whose nasty imagination?' said Isabel, going red down her neck.

'Yours,' said Nurse simply. 'And a lot of other silly gossips I could mention. I never did believe it from the start.'

'Oh, didn't you indeed! I'm surprised,' said Isabel, with impertinent emphasis.

Nurse actually let this pass, and hurried on to say in a different, confidential tone: 'But talk of nasty imaginations!...' and they went murmuring and hissing down the passage together.

Shortly after, Nurse said in a crisp yet off-hand way: 'Look here, you two – especially you, Sylvia – if you happen to speak to any of those children that hang around by the gate and they go telling you any nasty nonsense they've picked up, don't you take any notice. They may have got hold of some silly story or other that's been going about. I'm sure I don't know what they don't pick up, those children – nobody cares, more's the pity, and if I had my way—' She broke off, then added: 'Well now, you've heard what I say. If they repeat it, you just tell them there's nothing in it and never was and say I said so.'

'All right,' we said.

My mother went out about tea-time. As soon as the car had driven away with her, we made our way to the bottom of the garden, where Cissie and May were awaiting us. They said:

'The biby wasn't there.'

'Had the gipsies taken it away?'

'No. There wasn't no biby. She mide it all up.'

'! ! !'

'The p'liceman come to school this morning. 'E said for Chrissie to come along with 'im to show 'im the plice. Teacher was ever so upset. Chrissie didn't want to go. She fought 'im. She bit 'is 'and. But 'e took 'er along. When they got up to the pit, she took 'im to a plice and she says there, that's where it was. Well, it's not there no more, 'e says. It's gorn, she says. So 'e said for 'er to come along at once to the p'lice station. So she begun to take on and said she didn't want to go. Then she said there 'adn't ever been no biby. She'd mide it all up. So 'e brought 'er back and 'e told teacher she was a bad wicked little liar, wasting 'is time. So teacher mide 'er stand up in front of the 'ole class and tell us she'd mide it up. Teacher asked 'er what she wanted to tell such 'orrible wicked lies for. She never said nothink. She was shivering and shaking all over. So teacher took 'er into 'er own room and put 'er to sit down in a big chair with a rug round 'er, and she said she'd speak to 'er later. She's still there. Teacher's going to keep 'er there till 'er dad comes from work, and then take 'er back 'ome. Our mum says she's a bad bad girl and we're not to 'ave anythink to do with 'er. She says she 'ad ought to be sent to a re-formary.'

We never saw Chrissie again. The problems of her disgrace, her punishment, her future – all were kept from us; and even the know-alls of the lane were more or less in the dark about her destination when she vanished from the village.

We knew that our mother, ever combining prompt with humanitarian action, had taken charge of Chrissie's case. We did venture to ask Isabel whether it was true that Chrissie had been sent to a reformatory, but she said sharply, stuff and nonsense: Chrissie had gone right away to live with some kind people who loved her, and who would give her a mother's care and perhaps adopt her if she mended her ways and tried to be a good girl. She added: 'And if she grows up a decent ordinary being after all instead of a wild wicked demon, she'll have your mother's trouble and your father's generousness to thank for it.' So we knew that something impressive had been accomplished, and that our parents were paying for it.

This was before the days of child guidance clinics.

I remember only one or two more things about the Wyatts. Later on in October I plucked up courage to go past their cottage by myself: an act I had been unable to face since the death of Mrs. Wyatt. The lane was strewn with the drenched, honey drifts of poplar and chestnut leaves, and their sweet and pungent smell of death made my heart turn over. High over the fences of the little gardens, sunflowers flopped their harsh tawny faces. I came to the Wyatts' cottage, and Maudie was there, standing by the gate. One of her hands was bandaged and in a dirty sling; with the other she supported the baby who sat astride her crooked hip.

'Hallo,' I said timidly.

''Allo,' she said, unsmiling.

'What a lot he's grown,' I said.

She looked down at him and said in her indifferent way: 'Yes. 'E's getting on all right. 'E goes all over the place now.'

'Isn't he heavy for you to carry?'

'I don't mind. 'E likes a ride.' Suddenly she put her cheek down against his and cried: 'Don't you, ducks?'

He peeped out at me with a coy grin; then hid his face in her shoulder. A faint smile went over her face, maternal, indulgently mocking. He was bald, rickety, exactly like his brothers, but the hiding gesture reminded me of Chrissie; and what with that, and Mrs. Wyatt vanished for ever, and the desolate look of the cottage with Maudie standing alone there with the baby, and only two more to come home out of all the nine, I felt most terribly miserable and feared to disgrace myself by tears. I said:

'What have you done to your hand?'

'Got a poisoned thumb.'

'Does it hurt?'

'It throbs painful at nights. I 'ad it lanced but it goes on. The nurse comes to see to it. She says it got bad because it wasn't done up sooner. Still, I got to use it a bit – you can't do all your work with one 'and.'

I said I hoped it would soon be better, and then there was nothing more to say, and I said good-bye and went on. When I reached the corner I glanced over my shoulder, but she was not looking after me. Maudie had given up wanting anything I had got.

That winter they all went away. Mr. Wyatt got another job, over the other side of the country. I don't know if it was a better job. He came to say good-bye to my parents. I was not present during this interview, but later on, looking over the stairs, saw my father showing him out of the front door.

'Good-bye, Wyatt, my dear chap,' said my father warmly. 'The best of luck to you and yours.'

Mr. Wyatt went on wringing his hand, speechless, for a long time, then said brokenly: 'God bless you, sir,' and went away.

They left the cottage in such a state that it had to be fumigated and washed down with lysol from ground floor to attic. It stayed empty for a bit; then the landlord did a few repairs and put a coat of paint on, and another family came to live there. They planted vegetables and sowed a little plot of front lawn and cut out some little flower beds and made a little tile-bordered path to run exactly through the middle; and after a while it looked quite like the other cottages.

The Red-haired
Miss Daintreys

Much is said and written nowadays of the proper functions and uses of leisure. Some people, as we know, are all for the organisation of spare time. Some take exercise; some sleep; some wind up the gramophone; some lean against bars or mantelpieces. Others develop the resources of the intellect. I myself have been, all my life, a privileged person with considerable leisure. When asked how I spend it, I feel both dubious and embarrassed: for any answer implying some degree of activity would be misleading. Perhaps an approximation to the truth might be reached by stating that leisure employs me – weak aimless unsystematic unresisting instrument – as a kind of screen upon which are projected the images of persons – known well, a little, not at all, seen once, or long ago, or every day; or as a kind of preserving jar in which float fragments of people and landscapes, snatches of sound.

It is a detached condition. It has nothing of the obsessed egotism of daydreaming, and only a ghost of its savage self-indulgence. One might almost be dead, watching from the world of shades, so pure is one's observation, so freed from will, from the desire to shape or alter to personal ends. There is no drama in which one plays star-rôle; there is no emotion but that mild sort of satisfaction, based on familiarity and recognition, which one gets at the cinema, when the film turns out to be an enjoyable one seen several times before.

Yet there is not one of these fragile shapes and aerial sounds but bears within it an explosive seed of life. For most of us they will flit and waver by, and be gone again; but for a few, the shadowy and tranquil region which harbours their play is a working-place, stocked with material to be selected and employed. Suddenly, arbitrarily one day, a spark catches, and the principle of rebirth contained in this cold residue of experience begins to operate. Each cell will break out, branch into fresh organisms. There is not one of them, no matter how apparently disconnected, that is not capable of combining with the rest at some time or another.

Perhaps this is a wordy, unscientific way of describing the origins and processes of creative writing; yet it seems to me that nowadays this essential storing-house is often discounted, and that that is the reason for so much exact painstaking efficient writing, so well documented, on themes of such social interest and moral value, and so unutterably boring and forgettable. The central area has not been explored, and therefore all is dead. There is not a false word, nor one of truth.

I am surprised when authors have perfectly clear plans about the novels they are going to write; and I find it dismaying, for more reasons than one, to have the projected contents related to me, at length and in rational sequence. I would be more encouraged by such an answer, given in rather a hostile and depressed way, as: It is about some people; and if the author could bear to pursue the subject and mention any of the images and symbols haunting his mind – if he spoke for instance of a fin turning in a waste of waters, of the echo in the caves, of an empty room, shuttered under dust sheets, of an April fall of snow, of music from of the fair at night, of the burnt-out shell of a country house, that woman seen a moment from the bus top, brushing her long dark hair – I should feel that something was afoot. Writers should stay more patiently at the centre and suffer themselves to be worked upon. Later on, when they finally emerge towards the circumference they may have written a good novel about love or war or the class struggle. Or they may not have written a good novel at all.

But this is a far cry from the four red-haired Miss Daintreys, who lately, during one of these periods of idle leisure appeared, as through a trap-door, before my inward eye: four sisters with red hair, in blouses and skirts, sitting with their parents at breakfast in the dining-room of a seaside hotel, many years ago.

The room is vast. They loom a long way off, the other side of a no man's land of tables with white cloths and the smell of fried eggs, coffee and toast. They come punctually down to nine o'clock breakfast, and so does this other family, four children with their parents. I do not see them, but am one of them.

First one high startling stately figure, sailing like a figurehead; two more, advancing entwined, bearing down together; yet one more: fabulous sight. Each in turn bends to kiss first an old gentleman, then an old lady; takes her place at table. This table is in the window, and the August morning sun strikes in and kindles their crests into one blaze of blinding intensity.

My mother says to my brother: 'What would you like now, dear?' He is two, and replies in a loud coarse husky voice: 'A hegg.' Convulsions of shocked pleasure. Dropping his h's! What will they all think? – a common child. Apprehensively we glance over there. Their shoulders are shaking, then turn laughing faces. They are aware of us. They are of course admiring the blond curls of my brother; perhaps the juicy, up and coming appearance of all the four. Jolly-looking family.

After this the distance between the tables dwindles, vanishes. Subsequently we and the Daintreys will appear at the seaside in mixed groups and pairs.

Miss Mildred Daintrey. Miss Viola. Rosie and Dolly. Four daughters, all six foot or over.

Miss Mildred was the eldest, the family's chief prop and right hand, the unselfish one. She had a particularly large white face, narrow at the brows, broadening out like a pear, with rather pendulous cheeks. She wore pince-nez, and behind them her protuberant green eyes gleamed out with emotional benevolence. There was something marine about her appearance: that faintly phosphorescent flesh colour, like legs under water; that globularly soulful quality of the faces of fishes, mooning out from behind aquarium glass. She was no longer young, though it would appear now that she cannot have been elderly, as then seemed obvious. Her hair was the most uncompromising assertive red I have ever seen, and she wore it *en Pompadour*. The fact is, although she was so good and kind, that what with her height, her glasses, her phantasmagorical colouring, and her low, harsh, cockney-genteel voice, she was the picture of a horror-governess in a story by Mr. de la Mare. She gave the impression of one living in a state of perpetual self-dedication, almost of exaltation, due to her being so much in love with her family. Also she had a really tremendous feeling for kiddies, and it was she who set the whole thing going – established the contacts, clamped the bonds between the Ellisons and the Daintreys.

Next came Miss Viola, and I in my parallel position of second in the family felt for her the pangs of a particular sympathy: Not only this: she had established for herself beyond question the position I urgently coveted, of beauty of the family. Plunging once only into that fund of poetry that lurks in us all, Ma Daintrey, all Danäe to pre-Raphaelite influences, had achieved a flawless example of that movement – form, face, colour, name and all. My father admired her very much. She had a long curving goitrous neck and that incandescent skin that some red-haired people have, and long thickly fringed sandy-green eyes, and she did her hair I never could discover how in a low-lying amorphous swarming way over her ears and forehead, without a parting. She wore artistic clothes, peacock-blues and coppers, and she moved languidly, and her expression was ironical, *fin de siècle*. I don't know from what signs I deduced that her family feared as well as loved and admired her; that unlike the rest they knew her to be actuated by motives of private rather than group interest, and might prove a disintegrating force in the structure. She never took the initiative in those family demonstrations, those waist-entwinings, pats, pressures, cossetings, endearments, though she accepted all that came her way. Agreeable, dutiful, but cool; and generally thinking something or other funny. She was always the last down to breakfast, and after each meal she lit a cigarette: emancipated. They called her the independent one, but what this really meant was kept dark until friendship had definitely matured and then only revealed, I noticed, in an inhibited way. It was that she had Left Home, and shared a flat in Chelsea with a pal. I believe she had also a career, something in the nature of fashion-designing for a select few. Cold she was, but not virginal as was Mildred, or immaturely sex-conscious, like Rosie. How was I aware that her sexual experience was profound, curious, and that it separated her from her sisters? I suppose I was just young enough. A few years more, and *idées reçues*, from cousins chiefly, and the *Daily Mirror* serials, would have interposed between me and the subject.

Rosie and Dolly were twins. Rosie had a red face spattered with such a storm of dark freckles that her features such as they were were almost obliterated. She had an enormous bouncing bosom and her hips and calves sprang out like footballs. Given to bursts of breathy giggling, perfectly good-natured and self-satisfied, she was the jolly one of the family; also the athletic one. She played a smashing game of tennis in the period style for ladies, with low whizzing drives and half-volleys off the back line, and only an occasional portentous starchy forward swoop: none of those leaps, those upward flings and strains then known to be so unwise for girls; and of course covered from neck to just above ankle in stiff white *piqué*.

Dolly also was plump and freckled, but she did not play tennis. She did not do anything except sit with her parents and go for little strolls with Mildred, holding her hand. She seemed in the best of health, so it was puzzling to hear her referred to as the delicate one. Later we came to understand what delicate meant. Dolly was on the weak-minded side. Overhearing, as was my wont, from a cache in the shrubbery, conversations not intended for my ears, I learnt that this affliction was due to catastrophe at birth. Rosie turned up first, a bonny baby. A few hours later who should come along but Dolly, a surprise to all. Overcome with the shock, Ma Daintrey went off in a deep deadly faint. Back from the edge of the grave she was finally coaxed; but meanwhile, in the general agitation, Dolly, poor soul, had been dropped upon the floor, and Dolly grew up to be the home girl.

Ma Daintrey was immense, a monolith. When she sat she went down backwards all of a piece and there she stayed, semi-reversed, gasping, stuck, until she was pulled up again. Barely confined by taut black satin, her stomach protruded with monstrous abruptness, as if worn superimposed, a fertility symbol, to mark the pregnancies which had been her life's achievement. Her person expressed with overpowering force every kind of physical process. Even her voice, gassy, ruminative, replete, seemed a kind of alimentary canal and everything she said regurgitated. I remember when she spoke to us, or of us to our parents, how she seemed to swallow us down into her womanly amplitudes. She was prodigal of that kind of clucking indulgent pity whereby all manhood is castrated, the dignity of the intellect made naught, and humanity in general diminished to its swaddling-bands – the toy, pet, cross of suffering Woman.

Pa Daintrey was a very old gentleman, on the brink; he had heart trouble. Ma called him ducky and referred to him as her poor old dear. From him the girls inherited their height, and, one supposed, their pigmentation, but by this time he was totally bald. He had freckles on his huge old hands, freckles on his eyelids and ear-lobes, and a carbuncle on top of his head. Liver-coloured streaks and patches mingled with the freckles on a fungus-grey ground, forming an unappetising whole. He never spoke at all, not a word, nor, apart from an occasional flicker of a smile for Mildred, did he appear in any way receptive to the outer world. It was scarcely credible that he had once had the initiative to produce this giant brood who now enclosed him as a flourishing clump of red-hot pokers might enclose a decaying tree-stump. But initiative in every sense is exactly what once must have distinguished him; for – a point of no interest to me then – his career had been a romance of commerce. Starting as a suburban haberdasher in a very small way he had built up a great West End business, a store whose name was a household word. My mother had an account there. The Daintreys must have been extremely rich. I remember my parents saying so, and it was a surprise, for riches to me meant jewels, furs, silks, Rolls-Royces, a generally lavish style, and there was the reverse of this about the Daintreys. Their key-note was homely simplicity, and Ma was an inveterate postage-stamp remover. She kept a little second-hand store in her reticule, ready for further use.

Was this all of the Daintrey family? No, by no means. There was our boy Norman, in the business; and there was Gladys, our married girl.

They both came down one week-end and stayed in the hotel, Gladys with a husband called Arthur, Norman with a wife called Esmée and a couple of children called, yes, Peter and Wendy. We were impatient to see them, and hung around the pier as the four o'clock boat drew in. Our excitement was in the main scientific – a question of adding and classifying further specimens. Would the hair be red? We had bets on it. My undisciplined imagination led me to declare for red, red, red, but Jess said no, the idea of having six red-haired children was simply idiotic, and she proved to be right. Norman and Gladys were both dark and sallow, with opaque expressionless brown eyes; so that the question then arose; was red hair anti-matrimonial? Esmée was tiny, sharp and glittering, with a lacquered artificial appearance, black, white and vermilion; high heels and a lot of scent. She was the only one of them all in whom the riches seemed to come out. She was a real *de luxe* piece. The children were skinny and shrill, monkey-faced, a ravening predatory pair. Dancing on their toes in a perpetual nervous frenzy, they questioned, demanded, objected, entreated. They were precocious and self-possessed, and we thought them shockingly spoilt. They looked as if they could bite, and they did bite. We saw Wendy fasten her rat's teeth into the arm of their Swiss maid. The blood came, and Mariette retired holding a handkerchief to the place, silently weeping. Wendy went running away across the beach, and from a distance started to throw stones into the sea and kick up the sand. Nobody said anything.

Ma Daintrey sighed over her grandchildren and said their little brains were too forward and wore them out, but their mother seemed not to be worried. She took more notice of Norman, who was an excessively uxorious husband; he petted and pawed her and went on as if he were on his honeymoon. 'He worships her, Mrs. Ellison dear,' sighed Ma. It was a great man's weakness. What he went through when the children were born no tongue could tell. Pounds he lost in a single night – pounds. Another facer for me.

Gladys was a placid heavy character, weighted I thought with the consciousness of being the only married daughter. Whereas they were merely loyal and kind to Esmée, they doted on Arthur. He was short, broad, stout, pleased with himself. He had a popular line in wisecracks and gallant repartee. When after some sally they all surrounded and fell on him it seemed each time as if it must be the end of him, as if he must emerge married to another of them or to all of them. But out of all the blouses and hairpins he would bob up again sleek and tough, his small eyes snapping and beaming behind his rimless glasses, and go off well in control of the situation, with Gladys on his arm. They couldn't make a fool of him, they couldn't affect his jaunty masculinity. He'd picked Glad, the brunette; he'd meant to, and that was that. They'd been married five years. No little ones? No little ones, not even a Disappointment. It was a grief. But they were an ideal couple. Arthur was a real dear, the best of husbands. There was plenty of time.

Years later, I saw, in an exhibition of French nineteenth-century masters, a painting which stirred me with a peculiar excitement. My belief is that it was by Gauguin, and that it depicted a towering dark blue wave lifting within it the head and breast of a siren with red hair. Undine? All I remember – and this may be distorted by the passage of time and the violence of my feelings of the moment – is the prussian blue, snow-crested wave, a pale cheek laid sideways in it and that barbaric torch of red streaking up across the canvas. The literary, the supernatural elements in this odd work were perhaps enough in themselves to compel my imagination, for I was then an inveterate responder to the romantic in painting; but why that shock, personal, physical and confused? I think now that buried associations were struggling to live again, and that I was being confronted with some phantasy image of Miss Viola Daintrey against a background of summer sea. Not that any bathing photograph of her or any other of them comes back to me. I am sure I should have remembered them in bathing-suits. My belief is that none of them could swim. I know I got the notion that sea-water must be injurious to people of their complexion.

We ourselves were regular and methodical family bathers. My mother would wade out with my brother in her arms and stand waist high dipping him up and down. 'Boy splash sister! Splash! Sister won't splash Boy!' But it was no good. He did as he was told, directing a feeble spray from a limp reluctant paw at one or other of us, his face set grimly in suffering and disgust.

After a few moments he turned blue, his teeth started madly to chatter, and he was removed to his *Petit Beurres*. Then my father, setting an example of stylish limb-work, would swim out a short distance, and we would accompany him, a row of red rubber caps, competing with each other in the length and motive power of our Bath Club breast-strokes.

Peter and Wendy played on the breakwater, jumping from as high as they dared on to the sands. Stuck, Wendy screamed to be got down. I came hot foot from shrimping to assist her. She looked at me and her eyes went sharp and she said: 'I don't want you to lift me. I don't like your face much.' My arms dropped to my side. A murky tinge overspread the serene blue afternoon light, the caressing breeze scorched me with a sudden fan of flame. Could anyone have heard? In my ears her voice shrieked my murdered vanity from end to end of the bay. But nobody's head was raised to stare, no finger pointed. Children went on digging and running with buckets, nurses went on sitting with their bare feet stuck out in front, letting the sea air get at their corns. It was a convulsion of nature for me alone. I threw a few pebbles and took myself off – away from the beach, away from all creation. My back was aware of her, still standing on the breakwater watching me. As I started to climb the first steps up the cliff path I saw her, out of the corner of my eye, climb nimbly down and scamper away, spindly, fierce, a stinging insect contained in a shell of sponge-bag waders.

There was nobody in the hotel. Behind lowered sunblinds it dozed and all within was empty vistas and muffled reflections in brass and mahogany and my own figure, slipping across mirrors up the stairs. Furtively I shut the door of my bedroom and went to the glass. The face a child dislikes. Then I am ugly. At this period I wore a plate to straighten my teeth. Hitherto I had been proud of it, but now I deplored its glittering bar and hooks, and observed that it made my mouth protrude in an unpleasing way.

My nose was a lump, my eyes not blue, as I wished, but hazel. I thought too there was something sheepish and leering about my expression. A hate object, in a brown holland frock.

I looked out of the window and saw Ma and Pa Daintrey asleep in the garden, side by side in basket chairs. And doubtless their family were somewhere forming a convivial group; and my parents were taking a walk together, and my sisters were, I knew, making a seaweed garden together. Everywhere else was merrymaking and communion; I, I alone, was rejected and cast forth.

There was nothing to do but to embrace solitude. I would go up on to the downs and miss my tea. I went out along the turf walk, up the hill past the crazy grey house with turrets, and the square red house, so prosperous-looking, where a family of public schoolboys in white flannels held perpetual tennis-parties beyond cropped weedless lawns and beds of begonias, geraniums and antirrhinums; through the pine coppice and out on to the climbing cliff path which led through a place of brambles and gorse bushes to the heathery downs.

With some idea of hiding from the world I sought a shallow disused quarry overlooking the sea, and flung myself upon a bed of heather. Between the island and the mainland the sea was laid out like a length of blue silk. Features of the opposite coast were brought near and clear, as in a telescope: a solitary narrow white tower on the horizon; the spit of sand ending in a low sand-coloured castle where Charles I had been imprisoned; the mud flats between whose deeply scooped indentations the island boats churned in and out upon their brief journeys; the heavy woods lipping the flats' far rim. A long way below me the tide was out, and children bent with nets among the prawn-concealing rocks. That scarlet blob must be Sylvia, clambering in the struts of the lifeboat jetty, plunged, doubtless, in some megalomaniac dream of shipwreck and single-handed rescue.

Rob Roy canoes hovered close to the shore. Farther out a few small red and white sails crawled, paused, crawled on again. Once in a while something invisible seemed to skim the expanse of water, causing it to wrinkle and contract through all its surface. The *Duchess of Fife* emerged from behind the headland, plying her daily pleasure round, and was drawn across the middle distance.

The heather was springy beneath me, with a musical hiss like the last vibrations of a chorus of infinitesimal tambourines when I moved about on it. Gheen bugs and ladybirds laboured among the dry snapping roots. Heather is homely stuff, its wildness seems domesticated: because of the calendars and picture postcards, I suppose; and that cushiony toughness, like nursery furniture, made for wear and tear; and the amount of minute beetle and spider life that goes on in it. The smell is sweet too: it has a fresh cordial warmth and innocence.

All this combined to comfort me. That state, associated with mental anguish, of intense visual receptivity, gave way to lightness of spirit, and to a desire to make up some poetry. No sooner tapped than the facile fount began to flow. No trouble at all in those days. Heather, weather, brim, dim, bloom, gloom and off we go: every rhyme rhyming, every fairy flitting, stars glimmering, moon beaming, wind sighing, buds breaking – never stumped for a subject, never uneasy about a sentiment, each completed work as neat, tinkling and bland as a poem by Wilhelmina Stitch,[3] and quite satisfactory to myself.

Lying there in a trance of composition I beheld suddenly, some way off, a sight I had never seen before. It was simply my parents walking together. From over the crest of the down they came, down the winding turf path, shoulder to shoulder, a couple like any other couple. Totally unconscious of me, removed from me as if I saw them in a dream, familiar strangers, walking in a place that made a blank of me, cancelled my existence, in a place where they had been together before I was born... Here was I, there were they: my father with his Leander-ribboned panama and his stick, my mother with a white veil tied round her hat: no connection between us. What could they be talking about? They went by and disappeared behind a hedge of brambles.

I began to think there might be a snake somewhere near me in the heather. I could hear it rustling. Unnerved, bored now, resentful besides and hungry, I got up and started to hurry home; my one wish, to return as soon as possible to society; my fear, that by my mystifying absence I had isolated myself once and for all, and would never get back.

There they all were, sitting peacefully in the garden watching the sunset – my parents, the Daintreys, Jess and Sylvia. My brother had been removed to bed, and so had the demon children. With a ghastly attempt at nonchalance I emerged from the shrubbery and advanced towards them.

'Why, Rebecca, where have you been?' said my mother with calm affection.

'Just for a walk.' Strangled, sheepish voice.

'She looks flushed,' remarked Ma Daintrey; and there was that in her tone which hinted at consumption.

'Come along, old lady, take a pew over here by me,' said Miss Mildred.

I did so. I suppose the marks of crisis must have been apparent, for neither Jess nor Sylvia questioned me, not even afterwards; and after a few minutes my father looked across at me and winked.

Later that evening while Jess and I were brushing our hair for supper, there was a knock at the door, and Miss Mildred put her head in.

'Look here, you two old ducks,' she said, 'the kiddies want to say good-night to you. We can't get them to settle till they've seen you. Be dears and just pop in for a second.'

They were in their small beds, relaxed for once, harmless-looking, almost appealing in their sleeping-suits. They were on the look-out for us, and wriggled and simpered and rolled over on their backs like puppies as we approached.

'Good-night,' we said, embarrassed.

Jess took the plunge and bent down to kiss them. I followed suit, beginning warily with Peter. He flung up his arms and seized us in turn, violently, round the neck, clutching our heads to his. Now for the other one. Would she spurn me, bury herself, hit out at me? She flung up her arms and seized me violently round the neck, clutching my head to hers.

I often wondered afterwards if she planned this good-night episode to test the measure of my resentment or observe the extent of my afternoon's discomfiture. It could not have been the promptings of remorse.

Jess was the favourite of Miss Mildred. She would take Jess strolling along the turf walk or along the path that backed the beach and ran behind the bathing-huts. More than once, coming out of the voluptuous shop by the pier where the old gentleman with white side-whiskers sold marine objects – tropical shells and shell boxes and frames, and glass models of lighthouses filled with many-coloured sand – I would see them ahead of me; Jess's little waist encircled by the long arm of her companion, their back views – Miss Mildred's so large, stiff and military, Jess's so pliably and neatly turned – leaning sentimentally together. The look of them filled me with mixed scorn and envy. Jess would never refer to these times of communion. Probably the sloppiness made her self-conscious, but on the other hand to be thus distinguished caused her to feel grown-up and important. She always returned from these walks with a proud secretive curl to her lip. I expect Miss Mildred confided in her.

It was over poetry that Miss Mildred and I came together; for she also was a poet. One day she said to me:

'If you will show me your poems I will show you mine.'

Mine were written out in a black copybook, hers in a white vellum one, stamped with her monogram in gold. Her handwriting was exceptionally delicate, clear and pretty; mine was not. She liked my poems and I liked hers: we were twin songstresses. Her subjects were chiefly religious, but there were some about little children and about friendship, with a refined veiled glance at love. There were also a few humorous compositions which I passed over quickly, for I deplored light verse, thinking it *infra dig*. I was aware without a word said that she wished her works to be brought to the notice of my father, so I showed them to him. In his position of distinguished man of letters he was constantly being sent manuscripts for his advice and encouragement. He treated the authors – chiefly very young men and middle-aged ladies – in the same way as in my literary capacity he treated me – with unfailing sympathy and consideration. Never would he have crushed an aspirant as I at seventeen was crushed by a clever young man to whom I was rash enough to show a few chosen pieces. He said simply as he handed them back that they were like cream buns. During the course of my life I have had a woman's share of humiliation, but nothing has ever equalled the deadly effect of this. I am sure my father never told anyone their poems were awful. Once a lady called Marcia MacLanaghan sent him a slim volume called *Spindrift* with a long letter enclosed saying in a huge frantic slapdash hand: 'I had to *write out* my loneliness or DIE OF IT! ! !' This struck me forcibly: desperate remedies seemed called for; and I remember his sigh and comically rueful look when I anxiously inquired what reply he would make.

Miss Mildred's poems sprang from no such extremity; but there was no doubt, I knew it then, that she was a sad person in search of consolations. I do not know in what terms of cautious benevolence he complimented her, but I know that afterwards she looked extremely gratified, and said to me, wiping her glasses:

'Your father is my ideal of a gentleman.'

She was a great one for *vers d'occasion*. Upon my birthday, which fell during the holidays, I received by post a pale pink envelope addressed in her handwriting, and drew from it a pale pink scalloped gilt-edged card inscribed as follows, in a frame of hand-painted roses:

> *To Rebecca, on her eleventh birthday,*
> *Child of my heart, sing on! Thy childish song*
> *Makes sweet with melody the childish day;*
> *And when life's shadows fall upon the way*
> *The hearts that love thee best in love will pray*
> *That rose-strewn hours be thine thy whole life long.*
> M. D.

The effect of this was to inflate me. Child of my heart? I had thought this to be Jess. Sing on? Would I not! But the thought of thanking her suitably gave me a sickly feeling, and my mother had to do so for me, and did it in a deprecating style. My mother had many a subtle way of deflating vanity.

It was some time later that our Pekinese died and one of us wrote to acquaint Miss Mildred of the bereavement. She sent us by return of post an elegy, which my father read aloud to us. I know it hit about below the belt in a staggering way, but I can only recall the last three lines:

> *But perhaps far away*
> *Where wee angels play*
> *There's a corner for Mandy too.*

We all broke down, and Jess stormed from the room in indignant anguish and slammed the door.

A faint dubious memory returns to me of my father being instrumental in getting a piece of light verse of Miss Mildred's accepted by *Punch*, and of the great pride and pleasure this caused the Daintreys, and of my mother saying: 'Wasn't it a little rash?' – meaning would he not be deluged by her further efforts. But he never was. Miss Mildred was not my ideal of a lady, but she was one.

Miss Viola sat before the mirror in her bedroom, and I sat curled up on the bed watching her.

'I wish I had red hair like you,' I said.

Miss Viola smiled at herself, at me, mysteriously in the glass.

'My hair is auburn,' she said.

She took the pins out, let it fall down and started to brush it.

'May I look in your cupboard?' I said.

'Do.'

I opened the wardrobe and gloated at her dresses, hanging up long and limp in a row. She said:

'Which shall I wear to-night? You choose.'

I unhooked a copper-coloured one made of some heavy crêpe-like material, with a studded gold belt, and laid it on the bed.

'This one.'

'Oh, that's your favourite, is it?' She went on looking amused.

'You look beautiful in them all.'

'I designed this one,' she said. 'When you're a little older I'll design you a dress to wear to dinner parties. I believe you and I like the same things.'

'Can it be crimson?' I said.

'Yes, it can be crimson.'

She took off whatever she was wearing and stood up in a *broderie anglaise* petticoat and a camisole threaded with mauve ribbons. Her hair came round her shoulders. She looked absolutely unlike herself and I felt embarrassed.

'Could I be getting fat?' She smoothed her hips, looking in the glass.

'No, no.'

Everything I said came out in a strangled voice, and I had difficulty in breathing.

She poured out water in the basin and sponged her face, her neck, and her long strong-looking white freckled arms.

I watched her splashing and dipping and drying. I am sure no creams or lotions went on her face: nothing but water, and afterwards some powder on a big swansdown puff.

I said:

'I always have thought it's not very nice to be the middle one of the family... like you and me.'

'Really?'

'Yes, because you're not the eldest... and you're not the youngest...'

She paused in the act of twisting her back hair and looked at me thoughtfully in the glass.

'Yes,' she said. 'But on the other hand it's like the jam in a sandwich. Snug. You'll find there are advantages.'

'Have you found advantages?'

She nodded and smiled in the glass. She put on the copper dress over her head and the folds fell down round her and she fastened the gold belt round her waist. She looked like the illustrated princesses in the Andrew Lang[4] fairy books.

I said:

'Major Trotter's always following you about, isn't he?'

Miss Viola broke into a chuckle. That was what fascinated me most about her – her chuckle; and her low slow voice.

'You extraordinary creature!' Again she looked in the glass. 'I think he must be in love with you.'

She leaned back in her chair to laugh.

'Do you like him?' I said.

'Not in the least,' she said. 'Not in the – very – least.'

Major Trotter was a retired military gentleman with a heavy white moustache and a skin like that brown corrugated cardboard used for wrapping up books. He wore a spruce white duck suit, white suede brogues and a monocle. We thought him a very elegant figure of a gentleman. He was staying in the hotel and seemed lonely and on the prowl. He had made various attempts to enter into relations with the Daintreys, and I had noticed his monocle fixed in a business-like way upon the beauty of the family; but she never appeared even to see him. As a matter of fact it did not take him long to decide he was aiming too high. A few days later we observed that he had established contact with a high flat lady-like person from the other hotel. She was much taller than Major Trotter (he liked them so, one inferred) and had a gaunt outsize in faces, brightly rouged cheeks, fuzzy hair and a lot of large teeth in a rapacious non-shutting mouth. When he took her out boating she wore a flapping picture-hat. After that we scarcely saw him and when we did he took no interest in us.

Miss Viola took up a green scent-bottle, tipped it and dabbed the stopper behind each ear.

'Do you like the smell?' she said, bringing it over to me where I sat entranced, goggling, upon the bed.

'*Mm!*' She dabbed behind my ears. 'Is that the right place to put scent?'

'So they say.' She smiled. '*Dans la Forêt* it's called.'

Immediately dark green and scented glades enclosed us. By this time I was overcome by such a sense of excitement that I almost had to lie down on the bed; and what should she do next but light a cigarette and smoke it while she moved about the room, tidying things.

'One little puff before we dine,' she said. 'My respected Pa doesn't like it at all, at all. I try to spare his feelings.'

'Does your mother mind?'

She nodded, opening her narrow eyes at me.

'Ma thinks it'll be the death of me.'

'It won't, will it?'

I had never before seen a woman smoke and felt extremely disturbed.

'No, it won't.'

She stubbed out the cigarette and threw it far out of the window. She looked at me and chuckled again.

'Rebecca, Rebecca!' she said. 'Come along now.'

The Daintreys were great ones for organising expeditions. Once they took us all round the island in a coach and four. This was before the days of motor charabancs. There was a man beside the driver who blew a tune on a trumpet from time to time. I see Mildred and Viola, Rosie and Dolly, in straw hats and fresh white blouses, sitting with straight backs in a row behind the box. Their faces, warm with reflected sunlight, smile down at me as I clamber up.

We visited Carisbrooke Castle and saw the donkey turn the water-wheel, and after that we threw pebbles down a well and waited, counting, for the thin menacing splash and lugubrious echo at the bottom. We also visited Osborne House, but of its beauties and special features I remember nothing, for by this time I wanted badly to go somewhere and would not say so. I remember Miss Mildred murmuring at one point, 'Hadn't we all better take the opportunity?' – and everybody doing so except myself. Pressed further, I replied with a vehement negative, and Rosie said: 'She must be an angel,' and there was laughter. Once embarked upon this fatal course, I was obliged to hold to it, and my only other recollection of the outing is the torture I endured upon the long drive home.

Miss Mildred must definitely have enjoyed the society of children, for another time she asked my mother to let her take the whole lot of us, my brother included, over to the mainland to meet my father on a return journey from London.

It was always a pleasure to embark on one of those paddle steamers at the beginning or end of the holidays; but to be taking a pure joy ride, there and back, was a thing we had never thought of, and bore all the marks of a new and intense experience. The first pleasure was stepping over the gangway and finding oneself detached from land, testing the possibilities of another element; the second was the sound of churning paddles as we drew away from the pier; then came the satisfaction of seeing the shore recede, of picking out familiar objects – tents, people, houses, dogs – as they dwindled. Next we kept a sharp look-out for the Needles. When these impressive forms had been observed we were able to turn our attention to the boat itself.

Year after year, everything was the same: same ticket-collector, same stewardess, same smell of shrimps, brasso, red plush and Indian tea; same sailors in navy-blue jerseys with red initials on their chests. There was one in particular, large, with a genial, knobby raw-beef face and a flaxen curl quiffed up in the forefront of his sailor cap who was confused in my mind with Ham Peggotty.[5] A mystery was that as the boat neared land these Jolly Jack Tars always turned into porters, and said: 'Porter, madam?' and carried one's luggage. It seemed as if some accompanying physical transformation should have occurred; at least a porter's cap. It bothered us for years: were they porters? Were they sailors? Even the passengers showed only minute variations, for the same families came back summer after summer to the island.

Altogether the journey was so queer, so different from ordinary life, and yet with its unalterable features so familiar, that going on board was like re-reading a favourite story known by heart. There was the same sense of partaking in a creative experience: in something unreal and yet more real than life.

The rocking-horse movement of the boat caused my brother to become over-excited. He attracted attention by imbecile shouting and jumping, and made dashes to the side, flinging his burstingly stuffed legs alternately over the rail. Miss Mildred, who had a passive uncritical way with children, wasting no words and emanating an aura of firm serenity – perfect, I now think – removed him by hand to the first-class saloon. There she composed herself beside the window, gazing moonily at nothing, while he ran and rolled upon the red plush benches, or, clasping the pillars which supported the ceiling, let his lower limbs go and swirled drunkenly round and around them.

Unable to stomach the spectacle of our brother's release, we withdrew once more to the deck. There in the bows stood the boy who always stood in the bows. Clothed in navy-blue seaman's jersey and shorts, hands thrust in pockets, hair like frayed old rope, a drab nondescript grubby nosing dog's face. It seemed he travelled back and forth upon the steamer for ever, totally unattached. If one ventured to come and stand beside him, his extinct eye darted over one's head, he turned away with a wild tuneless snatch of whistling, stern and pre-occupied, as if the boat were his and might at any moment be rammed and founder. I wished to hear him speak, in order to discover whether or not he was a common boy; but I never did.

Now comes the best of the voyage, when the boat leaves the channel and begins to wind through ribbony deep-fretted flats to the pier and the harbour. Far over the expanses of glowing burnt sienna mud, a growth of luminous and tawny rice grass is blocked in as if with a palette knife. The same seagulls perch top-heavy upon the white stakes that mark the estuary's course; other waterfowl skim and scuttle across the marshes. Small sailing craft float past us running before the wind on a wing of red, white or tan sail. There, as usual, comes the sailing dinghy *Seamew*; the dark boy in a white public school sweater at the tiller; with him the fair pig-tailed girl in a green blazer: brother and sister, or maybe cousins, fortunate pair; and they are hero and heroine of an enthralling Book for Girls about a jolly pair of boy and girl chums, Jack and Peggy (Pegs), who charter a boat for the hols and have ripping adventures. They wave to us; we wave back: romantic moment. Receding, they stay fixed, an illustration, between blue water and blue sky, their crimson sail behind them. Till next summer, next summer...

There is the skeleton black hull, stuck on its side in the mud; and ah! there, a long way off, is that glimpse of a white house lifted up on a wooded slope, looking out across the estuary. To plunge into those bosomy secretive August woods, to be sealed up inside the core of that tender fecund blindness, to tunnel through it and be delivered out of it into open light and space, before that beneficent forbidding white façade: this is a latter-day interpretation of my violent and confused sensations about that symbolic landscape.

Now we are at the end of our journey. The paddles roar and thump. Noisily we back, advance, at last edge languidly up alongside the pier. Last pleasure: to watch the great coil of rope flung out across the dwindling strait, caught, pulled on, looped round the bollard. Now we are tied up and the paddles fall silent. Miss Mildred gathers us around her on deck, but Sylvia, tranced as usual, steps untimely forward upon the gangplank, and immediately begins to go down among a press of passengers and suitcases. 'Mind out, Missy!' calls Ham. Grinning, he retrieves her, picks her up, carries her on to the pier and sets her down with a flourish. Riding on his muscular arm, coy, blushing and confused, she, not I, is Little Em'ly.[6]

We sauntered up and down, waiting for the train to come in. There was nothing outstanding to look at, and Miss Mildred made no attempt to entertain us. Apart from dealing mildly and suitably with the infant caprices of my brother, she seemed dreamy, and I wondered if she was composing, or merely preparing herself, in wordless joy, for the sight of my father dismounting from his first-class compartment.

The little harbour described a shallow semi-circle. It was filled with pleasure craft at anchor and bordered by boat-building yards. Behind these the little town sat compact upon an incline. Smoke went up from household chimneys, hammering on wood sounded from the yards, the yachts, white, blue, red, green, bobbed at anchor and fluttered their flags. There was something festive, cosy and romantic about the scene; as if a life of small shops and lamps and teapots in back parlours, of church and chapel-going and allotments were blended with a life setting towards departures and the open sea; yet all the separations must be brief, the journeys domestic and propitious; and the people must be contented yet lightly restless, their sober pedestrian land rhythm just shaken by a tremor of the emotional swing of tides and gulls.

It was not long before the London train appeared, and out stepped my father, looking, as he always did, very much amused when he saw us, and doffing his hat to Miss Mildred with such stylish grace that I felt she must find it wonderfully gratifying. The high spot of the trip was still before us: tea on the boat going back. Bread and butter, shrimps, raspberry jam, Dundee cake, Mazawattee tea – tea the colour of Guinness, fiercer and more bitter than any I have tasted since, even at Paddington, or at Women's Institute tea-parties. The weather had become chilly and overcast, and we remained below and played I Spy – with colours, not the alphabet, so that my brother could join in. When we got back Miss Mildred told my mother we had been models and a pleasure to take out.

This is all I can remember about the Daintrey family at the seaside.

Then there was a Sunday when some of them came down from London in an enormous hired Daimler to spend the day with us at our home by the river. It was a very hot day, and I see Ma in black satin prone in a garden chair beneath the walnut tree, fanning herself and gasping. I see Pa beside her. His lips a lurid blue, his hands shaking, completely silent, he seems in the inner-most recess of his exhausted being to be intent on preserving the last flicker of himself. I remember a moment when, suddenly, the paralysis of alarm began to strive with the smiles of hospitality upon my mother's features. What if they both died upon her hands before the day was out? She said later to my father: 'It was a great mistake.' These words rang painfully in my ears: I had assumed that having the Daintreys must be pure pleasure for all; it was not so. Children savour the company of their favourites with a simple direct and intemperate zeal which leaves no room for so chilling a concept as social inconvenience. To discover that the objects of one's enthusiasm have been in the adult view merely a bore, or troublesome, is more than upsetting, it is shocking. It causes a sinking, almost nausea, like the first mutter of a thunderstorm, or the suspicion of cruelty in the world.

Curiously, I remember nothing about the girls that day. Two came. One was certainly Miss Mildred, for it was on that occasion that we were each presented with a little attaché case stamped with our initials: Jess's was blue, Sylvia's green, mine red. I still have it. I trace her by the gift, but cannot see her. Is it Viola or some other swan-like young woman – for they abounded, in white, with parasols, by the river in those days – standing on the bank, her face under a wide straw hat lucent with reflected light, watching the swans as they come hissing to the raft? This must be towards evening when it grew cooler, and Pa and Ma were conducted down to the boathouse to watch us swim. Ma said we were pretty dears; the sight of our bonny limbs seemed to cause her sorrow and foreboding. She felt Sylvia's calves and said with a sigh: 'She's very firm.' She asked my mother whether she felt quite happy about the effects of immersion upon us in our overheated condition. She herself never trusted river water. The only son of a dear widowed cousin of hers had swallowed a fatal mouthful of bacteria while bathing. He was gone in a week.

The wax-skinned reed-pierced olive river flowed by, carrying the swans, and the skiffs and punts, and the incandescent midge-swarms. Oars thudded in rhythm, blades tore the polished surface silkily, an excursion steamer went by crammed with people dancing on deck to the thump of a strident piano. They leaned over the side and waved. A man's voice shouted: 'Hallo, Grannie!' Then the glittering wash came running in level waves and smacked the bank and gurgled beneath the raft. Incongruous element in the light, shifting scene, the black bulk of old Mr. and Mrs. Daintrey sat on the boathouse bench, shored up with cushions in the cool of the evening.

'We're a happy family,' she sighed, plunged in her inner vision. 'They're all very good children to their old Ma and Pa.'

She took up Pa's crumbling, speckled-fungus hand, and held it in hers.

We went next summer to the island. It was the last week in July, 1914. The Daintreys were to come in August. On August 5th the shore was totally deserted. Acting upon the assumption that the German fleet would immediately steam up the Channel and open fire upon the bay, everybody had fled to the mainland. We stayed on and had our holiday much as usual. Of the world crisis I remember only that sudden emptiness of the beach and the expression on my father's face as he sat reading the papers all day, and his saying to my mother: 'It'll be over by Christmas.' Khaki figures and barbed-wire entanglements appeared round the fort on the downs. Battleships steamed by, gun practice shook us several times a day, once or twice an aeroplane bumbled across the straits and toppled about and landed for a few hours. Sylvia and I spent a long broiling afternoon stalking a German spy who turned out to be a well-known elderly author walking over from his house in Freshwater Bay to visit my parents. We waited for the Daintreys, but they did not come. The island never saw them as a family again.

Did we ever see them thus again? Yes, once. At Miss Mildred's wedding.

It was in the middle of the war years that she wrote to tell us that she was engaged to be married. She was doing war work in some Government office, and he was the head of her department and love had gradually grown up between them. She called him her man and said she was very, very happy and might she bring him down to lunch one Sunday?

They came; and the shock was that he was remarkably handsome, like a diplomat on the stage: tall, faultlessly dressed, with wavy grey hair and regular features. His name was Mr. Martin Chisholm, and he was a widower. We expected to see Miss Mildred transformed into something more like the popular notion of a bride, but no, she was exactly the same, only worse if anything, so to speak. She had aged and looked worn and lined and paler than ever. Pince-nez still clasped her nose, her hair was combed up in the same governessy way and her hat was frumpish. We did not really see how he could so discredit himself. We valued Miss Mildred, but we deplored his taste. And love beautified, we knew: it was a worry. I thought then in a confused way that the effort of pulling off so sensational a coup, the aim and hope, long-deferred, of her life, had taken it out of her to the point of exhaustion. We watched avidly for signs of passion, and in so far as, nourished on *Daily Mirror* serials, we expected burning glances, mingling of hands, kisses behind the shrubbery, we were doomed to disappointment. Two or three times we did see them exchange a gentle resting look and smile. It seemed like mere affection, not romance; and though this was a blow for us, we had to admit that anything more violent would have been unsuitable.

In the afternoon, we tactfully allowed them to stroll round the garden, arm in arm. I thought: for the rest of her life she will have someone always to stroll with arm in arm. Later she came back smiling and drew Jess and me forth with her through the french windows, while Mr. Chisholm stayed behind and had a nice chat with my parents. 'I want them to get to know him,' she said. She put an arm round each of us, and thus entwined we wandered in loving converse, and everything was as usual. She asked us what we thought of him and we replied with embarrassment that he was very handsome, and she said with soft intensity: 'Yes, and better than handsome.' She told us what dears he thought us all: he'd summed us up already – Jess the sensible one, me the dreamy one, Sylvia the deep one – as she had known he would. She said his dear wife had died many years ago, and since then he had been so lonely, so unhappy. She was going to do her best to make it up to him now. She wanted us all to be great friends always. She had hoped to have us as bridesmaids, it had always been one of her dearest wishes, but owing to the war it must be a very quiet wedding and, though of course we must all be there to see her married, only wee Wendy and Peter would follow her to the altar. After war was over, and that must be soon, they were going on a long voyage, out to China where he had lived and worked as a young man. Then they would come back and settle in the country, and we were to come and stay with them, in turns, often and often.

After tea they went back to London. When she said good-bye to my mother she held her by both hands and said: 'You know, we're very sure'; and to my father she said with an extraordinary simple trustful smile: 'I knew you'd be glad of my happiness.' As for Mr. Chisholm he did what was fitting by wringing our hands hard and saying with warmth, in reply to my parents' parting expressions of congratulation: 'I am a very lucky man.'

Afterwards I overheard them discussing Mr. Chisholm. There was surprise in their voices while they rehearsed his qualities: well-read, travelled, good-looking, intelligent: a notable man. 'What do you suppose…?' said my mother dubiously. My father shrugged his shoulders, looking amused. Knowing that our ears were agog they dropped into veiled and laconic allusions: nest-feathering, eyes to the main chance, and other financial circumlocutions. It had never occurred to me that Miss Mildred might be cynically wooed for her money: I now understood it to be so.

'Poor woman,' said my father. 'Her face is not her fortune.'

'Dear me, how plain she looked.' My mother sighed. 'And such a bad colour. I don't believe she's strong. I wonder what her age is. Nearly forty, I imagine.'

'Well, I wish the old girl luck with all my heart,' said my father. 'She'll make him a dashed good wife.'

Next month the wedding.

War-time it may be and concessions have to be made in the matter of bridesmaids, but Miss Mildred is determined to have a memorable ceremony: St. Margaret's, full choral, lilies, white satin and all. Conscious of our wedding coat and hats we enter the church along a strip of red carpet; we catch a glimpse of Wendy and Peter in Kate Greenaway[7] garb, fidgeting and gnawing about in the shadows just inside, guarded by a sharp shiny black and vermilion wing that is Mrs. Norman; we see our boy Norman and our Arthur stepping forward, beaming, in morning dress, to conduct us to our seats: they seem to be in unnaturally high spirits, and I am surprised at this, but understand it now. We observe group after group of strangers noiselessly slipping into the places. We are impressed by the sight of old Mrs. Daintrey prone in a front pew, flowing with veils and chains and tears; of Rosie and Dolly beside her, looking patchy, woeful and bemused; of the graceful back and shoulders of an elegant woman sitting beside them, but with a suggestion of being separated from them. Slowly she turns her head and winks at us and it is Viola. The decorations consist of arum lilies and poinsettias in profusion: a winter wedding. The organ is pealing. Mr. Chisholm emerges from nowhere and stands waiting by the steps. At this, Ma Daintrey's sobs redouble. Manly, superbly dressed, controlling emotion, he whispers to his best man, steps forward and bows over Ma gravely, with a filial kiss – damp for him – steps back to his place. Far down at the end of the aisle there is a stir; a lot of white and singing is coming up towards us. It is the choir; and, oh, goodness, following them, a fluid floating column of white, a long formal column of black: it is the bride upon the arm of her father. Miss Mildred, what has happened to you? She is transfigured, she is a Beauty. My throat contracts as she passes, her face half smiling behind the white veil covering it. She carries a white prayer-book and she has removed her pince-nez, and she has been visited by a hairdresser who has done her hair low, close to her head, with a middle parting and soft waves. The veil has toned down the ginger to a tender brilliance. She wears a wreath of orange blossom, and you see that thus bound the shape of her head is beautiful. Also her body moulded in white satin looks young, noble and supple. Pa Daintrey is ashen, and there is an alarmingly collapsed look about him, yet he holds himself upright and paces on with unfaltering tread; he will get through it somehow and do them credit on this his last public appearance. As they pass the family pew Miss Mildred turns her head, and the most loving smile imaginable shines out of the veil on to the weltering mass of Ma. On they go. Now Mr. Chisholm, looking upset and no wonder, steps forward to meet his bride. The procession stops. The bridal pair stand shoulder to shoulder before a waiting surplice. Wendy and Peter lay down the long satin train and stand at either corner of it, scratching themselves from time to time and frowning at each other. Pa Daintrey having inaudibly delivered over his favourite daughter to her bridegroom, retires with stricken dignity to take his place beside her mother. A slow tear trickles down his long cheek and slowly he takes out a handkerchief and wipes it away. Ma takes his hand; and through the remainder of the ceremony she goes on stroking and patting it. The ritual proceeds. I cannot get it out of my head that Miss Mildred is a victim, and am unnerved by the pathos of the back view of her patient sacrificial white form. The ring is on. Her train sweeping majestically behind, they move forward alone to the altar, where another surplice receives them and begins to say something urgent and confidential in their private ear. We kneel, we rise, it is all over, they vanish into the vestry and so do the Daintrey family and some strangers on the opposite side of the aisle. Led by the choir we occupy ourselves in their absence by singing 'O Perfect Love.' Then they all come back. The organ bounces into the opening bars of the Wedding March, and down the aisle comes the radiant Miss Mildred on the arm of Mr. Chisholm.

Her veil is now thrown back, it is her own face and none other blinking without the pince-nez; but she looks so cheerful, rejuvenated and triumphant that the illusion almost persists. She has brought it off, she is a married woman, she has entrusted herself to the love of a good man.

We go to the reception and are announced by a stentorian butler, and find Miss Mildred and Mr. Chisholm arranged as a group in the middle of a very large room. She kisses us warmly but absent-mindedly as we file past in the middle of a long procession of wedding guests. Mr. Chisholm seems pleased to see us and wrings our hands to the bone. My mother has told us to say: 'Congratulations,' but naturally this is impossible and we can only look up at them with sheepish smiles. We are given an insufficient helping of wedding cake and manage to spot our coffee set and card among the lordly array of wedding gifts. There is a moment when I see Miss Mildred with unknown friends around her, a champagne glass in her hand, throwing her head back to laugh in the jolliest way. It is the first time I have ever seen her laugh.

She did enjoy her wedding.

And that was the last time we saw the Daintreys. It was about then that my father embarked uncomplainingly upon the long course of his last illness, and we ceased to invite friends for week-ends.

I do not know how long it was after that – a year? – more? – the war was over – that my mother came to us with a serious face and a letter in her hand edged with black, portentous. 'Girls, you remember the Daintreys –' She looked and sounded terribly sorry. I recognised Ma Daintrey's handwriting, which was strong, educated, flowing. Bad news. Miss Mildred was dead. Taken ill on the way back from China. Buried at sea.

We knew that they had carried out that cherished plan because she had faithfully sent us post-cards. No doubt she was on her way back to find her country home when death overtook her. Years of peace and contentment were ahead of her; but she had died, and been pitched overboard from the deck of a P. & O. liner. Vividly her family in bereavement were conjured up before us: the tears, the broken-hearted tears, the horror-struck unbelief, the Christian resignation. The aching void that none can fill. God's will be done. She has gone before, she is waiting on the other side. Our right hand, so loving, the best of daughters, happiest of wives. Her husband, poor dear, another son to us, we must think of him. We all try to help one another, the dear remaining girls are very good, but my poor old dear is quite broken: his favourite daughter. We were such a happy family.

It was not till later that I somehow gleaned that it was her final attempt to fulfil herself – to be a mother – that had killed her. She was over forty, not healthy – she could not pull it off. She sickened in the early months of her pregnancy, succumbed in wretched suffering to some illness incident to childbearing. I hear her murmur on her deathbed, like Charlotte Brontë: 'Oh! I am not going to die, am I? He will not separate us, we have been so happy.'

Later there was a brief letter from Mr. Chisholm thanking my parents for condolences. Miss Mildred had loved us so much, he said; he was grateful for our sympathy. She had so sweetened his days, life was empty without her. He must live on memories now, and thank God they were all cloudless ones. He sounded dreadfully unhappy. We thought for such a handsome man to be twice a widower was too much bad luck: it seemed almost like a curse. It was clear that the suspicions of my parents were quite unfounded: it had been a marriage of true minds, and her plainness and her money had proved no obstacles whatever. I am sure now that Miss Mildred, despite her sentimentality had enough goodness and instinctive truth in her not to deceive herself about essentials.

Only the other night I re-read a volume of stories called *Rhapsody* by Dorothy Edwards[8] and came upon these words:

'There is something very attractive about the thought of the skeletons of red-haired people'; and I thought of the white bones of Miss Mildred picked by the currents of the Indian Ocean.

We were all very sorry; but we were growing up now; the Daintreys belonged to our childhood and had grown a little dim. I think Pa died soon after: I remember another envelope inch-deep in black. Dignified with the title of beloved husband, her poor old dear went peacefully in his sleep to join Miss Mildred. Her prayers had been granted: he had been taken first, spared the last grief and loneliness. Never a harsh word in fifty years of perfect married life. Once more the dear girls were being very good.

Then Ma died. I suppose we wrote and were written to, but I do not remember anything of that. The curtain falls definitely for the last time.

What happened to the rest, I wonder?

When I count up and find that Viola must be a woman nearing fifty I feel extremely surprised; and it is a measure of the mad view which children have of adults that whether I think of her as married to an artist or a stock broker, as a business woman or a spiritualist medium, as vanished to live with the Indians in New Mexico or sharing a country cottage in Surrey with a fellow spinster, each picture seems equally possible yet utterly unfitting.

I see Rosie in uniform, red and portly, pretty high up in the Women's Territorials. Gladys and Arthur, Norman and Esmée must be getting on. I dare say poor Dolly is shared out between them, and does little jobs about the house.

Doubtless Wendy and Peter managed somehow to expand their frames and grow up to look and behave much like other people: but not in the least like their relations of the two former generations. Product of an expanding age, the mould is broken that shaped and turned those out. Forced up too rapidly, the power in them, so lavish and imposing as it seemed, sank down as rapidly and faded out. There will be no more families in England like the Daintrey family.

When the Waters Came

Very long ago, during the first winter of the present war, it was still possible to preserve enough disbelief in the necessity for disaster to waver on with only a few minor additions and sub-tractions in the old way. The first quota of evacuated children had meant a tough problem for the local ladies; but most of them, including her own, had gone back to London. Nothing very disturbing was likely to happen for the present. One thought, of course, of sailors freezing in unimaginable wastes of water, perhaps to be plunged beneath them between one violent moment and the next; of soldiers numb in the black-and-white nights on sentry duty, crammed, fireless, uncom-forted on the floors of empty barns and disused warehouses. In her soft bed, she thought of them with pity – masses of young men, betrayed, helpless, and so much colder, more uncomfort-able than human beings should be. But they remained unreal, as objects of pity frequently remain. The war sprawled every-where inert: like a child too big to get born it would die in the womb and be shovelled underground, disgracefully, as monsters are, and after a while, with returning health and a change of scene, we would forget that we conceived it. Lovers went on looking on the bright side, stitching cosy linings, hopeful of saving and fattening all the private promises. The persisting cold, the catastrophes of British plumbing, took precedence of the war as everybody's topic and experience. It became the political situation. Much worse for the Germans, of course. Transport had broken down, there was no coal in Berlin. They'd crack – quite likely – morale being so low already.

The climax came one morning when the wind changed, the grey sky let out rain instead of snow. Then, within an hour, the wind veered round again to the north, the rain froze as it fell. When she went into the kitchen to order the day's meals, the first of the aesthetic phenomena greeted her. The basket of vegetables had come in folded in a crust of ice. Sprouts, each crinkled knob of green brilliance cased in a clear bell, looked like tiny Victorian paperweights. The gardener scratched his head.

'Never seen nothink like it in fifty years. Better be careful walking out, 'M. There'll be some broken legs on the 'ill. It's a skating rink. I slipped up a matter of five times coming along. Young Bert's still trying to get up to the sheep at the top. He ain't done it yet.' He chuckled. 'It's a proper pantomime. The old Tabbies'll have to mind their dignities if they steps out to-day.'

The children ran in with handfuls of things from the garden. Every natural object had become a toy: twigs, stones, blades of grass cased in tubes of ice. They broke up the mounds, and inside were the smooth grooved prints of stems and leaves: a miracle.

Later she put on nailed shoes and walked with difficulty over the snowy field path to the post office. The wind was a steel attack; sharp knobs of ice came whirling off the elms and struck her in the face. She listened by what was once a bush of dogwood, now a glittering sheaf of long ice pipes that jangled and clashed together, giving out a musical ring, hollow, like ghostly xylophones.

At the post office, the customary group of villagers was gathered, discussing the portents, their slow, toneless, deprecating voices made almost lively by shocked excitement. The sheep in the top field had been found frozen to the ground. Old Mrs. Luke had slipped up on her doorstep and broken her thigh. The ambulance sent to take her to hospital had gone backwards into the ditch and overturned. Pigeons were stuck dead by their claws on branches. The peacock at the farm had been brought in sheathed totally in ice: that was the most impressive item.

'I *wish* I'd seen it!'

Stiff in its crystal case, with a gemmed crest, and all the blue iridescence gleaming through: a device for the birthday of the Empress of China.

That night was the end of the world. She heard the branches in the garden snapping and crashing down with a brittle rasp. It seemed as if the inside of the earth with all its roots and foundations had become separated from the outside by an impenetrable bed of iron; so that everything that grew above the surface must inevitably break off like matchwood, crumble and fall down.

Towards dawn the wind dropped and snow began to fall again.

The thaw came in February, not gradually but with violence, overnight. Torrents of brown snow-water poured down from the hills into the valley. By the afternoon, the village street was gone, and in its stead a turbulent flood raced between the cottages. The farm was almost beleaguered: water ran through the back door, out the front door. The ducks were cruising under the apple trees in the orchard. Springs bubbled up in the banks and ditches, gushed out among roots and ivy. Wherever you looked, living waters spouted, trickled, leaped with intricate overlapping voices into the dance. Such sound and movement on every hand after so many weeks of silence and paralysis made you feel light-headed, dizzy; as if you, too, must be swept off and dissolved.

'Oh, children! We shall never see the village looking like this again.'

She stood with them at the lower garden gate, by the edge of the main stream. There was nobody in sight.

'Why not?' said John, poking with the toe of his Wellington at the fringe of drifted rubbish. 'We might see it next year. No reason why not if we get the same amount of snow.'

Where were all the other children? Gathered by parents indoors for fear of the water? The cottages looked dumb. 'It's like a village in a fairy story.'

'Is it?' said Jane, colouring deeply. 'Yes, it is.' She looked around, near and far. 'Is it safe?'

'Of course it's safe, mutt,' said her brother, wading in. 'Unless you want to lie down in the middle of it and get drowned.'

'Has anything got drowned, Mummy?'

'No. The cows and horses are all safe indoors. Only all the old dead winter sticks and leaves are going away. Look at them whirling past.'

The water ran so fast and feverish, carrying winter away. The earth off the ploughed fields made a reddish stain in it, like blood, and stalks of last year's dead corn were mixed and tumbled in it. She remembered *The Golden Bough*,[9] the legend of Adonis, from whose blood the spring should blossom; the women carrying pots of dead wheat and barley to the water, flinging them in with his images. Sowing the spring.

The children ran along the top of the bank, following the stream, pulling sticks from the hedge and setting them to sail.

'Let's race them!'

But they were lost almost at once.

'Mummy, will they go to the sea?'

'Perhaps. In time.'

Jane missed her footing and slithered down into the ditch, clutching at John, pulling him after her.

'It's quite safe!' he yelled. 'It only comes half-way up her boots. Can't we wade to the cross-roads and see what happens?'

'Well, be terribly careful. It may get deep suddenly. The gravel must be washing away. Hold her hand.'

She watched them begin to wade slowly down away from her, chattering, laughing to feel the push and pull of the current at their legs.

'It's *icy*, Mummy! It's lovely. Bend down and feel it.'

Moving farther away, they loosed hands and wandered in opposite directions, gathering up the piles of yellow foam-whip airily toppling and bouncing against every obstruction. She saw Jane rub her face in a great handful of it.

Oh, they're beginning to look very far away, with water all round them. It can't be dangerous, I mustn't shout. They were tiny, and separated.

'Stay together!'

She began to run along the bank, seeing what would happen; or causing it to happen. It did happen, a moment before she got there. Jane, rushing forward to seize a branch, went down. Perfectly silent, her astonished face framed in its scarlet bonnet fixed on her brother, her Wellingtons waterlogged, she started to sink, to sway and turn with the current and be carried away.

'How could you... John, why didn't you?... No, it wasn't your fault. It was mine. It wasn't anybody's fault. It's all right, Jane! What a joke! Look, I'll wrap you in my fleecy coat, like a little sheep. I'll carry you. We'll hurry home over the field. We'll be in hot baths in ten minutes. I'm wet to my knees, I've got ice stockings – and all of Jane is wet. How much of John is wet?'

'None of me, of course,' said John, pale and bitter. 'Have *I* got to have a bath?'

An adventure, not a disaster, she told herself unhopefully, stumbling and splashing up towards the garden over the ploughed field, weighed into the earth with the weight of the child, and of her ever more enormous clogged mud-shoes that almost would not move; and with the weight of her own guilt and Jane's and John's, struggling together without words in lugubrious triangular reproach and anxiety.

But by the end of the day it was all right. Disaster had vanished into the boothole with the appalling lumps of mud, into the clothes-basket with sopping bloomers and stockings, down the plug with the last of the mustard-clouded bath water. Jane lay wrapped in blankets by the nursery fire, unchilled, serene and rosy. John toasted the bread and put on his two yodelling records for a celebration. Adventure recollected in tranquillity made them all feel cheerful.

'I thought I was done for that time,' said Jane complacently.

'It'll take more than that to finish you – worse luck,' said John, without venom. 'We haven't had a moment's peace, any of us, since you were born. To-morrow I'm going to make a raft and see how far I can get.'

'I'm afraid by to-morrow it'll all be dry land again.'

She looked out of the window and saw that the water in the fields had almost disappeared already. After countless white weeks, the landscape lay exposed again in tender greens and browns, caressing the eye, the imagination, with a promise of mysterious blessing. The air was luminous, soft as milk, blooming in the west with pigeon's breast colours. In the garden the last of the snow lay over flower-beds in greyish wreathes and patches. The snowman stood up at the edge of the lawn, a bit crumpled but solid still, smoking his pipe.

What will the spring bring? Shall we be saved?

'But you were wrong about one thing, Mummy,' said Jane, from the sofa. 'You know what you said about... you know.'

'About what?'

'Go *on*. Cough it up.'

'About nothing being... you know,' said Jane with an effort. 'Drowned.'

'Oh dear, was I wrong?'

'Yes, you were wrong. I sor a chicking. At least, I think so.'

A Dream of Winter

In the middle of the great frost she was in bed with influenza; and that was the time the bee man came from the next village to take the swarm that had been for years buried in the wall of her country house; deep under the leads roofing the flat platform of the balcony outside her bedroom window.

She lay staring out upon a mineral landscape: iron, ice and stone. Powdered with a wraith of spectral blue, the chalky frost-fog stood, thickened in the upper air; and behind it a glassy disc stared back, livid, drained of heat, like a gas lamp turned down, forgotten, staring down uselessly, aghast, upon the impersonal shrouded objects and dark relics in an abandoned house. The silence was so absolute that it reversed itself and became in her ears continuous reverberation. Or was it the bees, still driving their soft throbbing dynamo, as mostly they did, day in, day out, all the year round? – all winter a subdued companionship of sound, a buried murmur; fiercer, louder, daily more insistent with the coming of the warm days; materialising then into that snarling, struggling, multiple-headed organism pinned as if by centripetal force upon the outside of the wall, and seeming to strive in vain to explode away from its centre and disperse itself.

No. The bees were silent. As for the children, not one cry. They were in the garden somewhere: frost-struck perhaps like all the rest.

All at once, part of a ladder oscillated across the window space, became stationary. A pause; then a battered hat appeared, then a man's head and shoulders. Spying her among the pillows, his face creased in a wide grin. He called cheerfully: 'Good-morning!'

She had lost her voice, and waved and smiled, pointing to her throat.

'Feeling a bit rough? Ah, that's a shame. There's a lot of nasty colds and that about. Bed's the best place this weather, if you ask *me*.'

He stepped up on to the little balcony, and stood framed full-length in the long sash window – a short, broad figure in a roll-collared khaki pull-over, with a twinkling blue small peasant's eye in a thin lined face of elliptical structure, a comedian's face, blurred in its angles and hollows by a day's growth of beard.

'Come to take that there swarm. Wrong weather to take a swarm. I don't like the job on a day like this. Bad for 'em. Needs a mild spell. Still, it don't look like breaking and I hadn't nothink else on and you wanted the job done.'

His speech had a curious humming drawl, not altogether following the pattern of the local dialect: brisker, more positive. She saw that, separated by the frosty pane, they were to be day-long companions. The lady of the house, on her bed of sickness, presented him with no problems in etiquette. He experienced a simple pleasure in her society: someone to chat to on a long job.

'I'll fetch my mate up.'

He disappeared, and below in the garden he called: 'George!' Then an unintelligible burr of conversation, and up he came again, followed by a young workman with a bag of tools. George felt the embarrassment of the situation, and after one constricted glance through the window, addressed himself to his task and never looked towards her again. He was very young, and had one of those nobly modelled faces of working men; jaw, brows profoundly carved out, lips shutting clearly, salient cheekbone, sunk cheek, and in the deep cavities of the eye-sockets, eyes of extreme sadness. The sorrow is fixed, impersonal, expressing nothing but itself, like the eyes of animals or of portraits. This face was abstract, belonging equally to youth or age, turning up here and there, with an engine driver's cap on, or a soldier's; topping mechanics' overalls, lifting from the roadmender's gang to gaze at her passing car. Each time she saw it, so uncorrupted, she thought vaguely, romantically, it was enough to believe in.

She had had a lot of leisure in her life to look at faces. She had friends with revolutionary ideas, and belonged to the Left Book Club.

'Be a long job this,' called the bee man. 'Looks like they've got down very deep.'

A sense of terror overcame her, as if some dreaded exploratory physical operation of doubtful issue, and which she would be forced to witness, was about to take place. This growth was deep down in the body of the house. The waves of fever started to beat up again.

The men disappeared. She waited for the children to appear upon the ladder; and soon, there they were. John had taken the precaution of tucking his sister's kilt into her bloomers. In his usual manner of rather disgusted patience, he indicated her footing for her. They pranced on the balcony, tapped on the pane, peered in with faces of lunatic triumph, presenting themselves as the shock of her life.

'A man's come to do the bees!'

'It's perfectly safe,' yelled John, in scorn, forestalling her. But voiceless, she could only nod, beam, roll her eyes.

'Shall we get Jock up?'

Frantically she shook her head.

'But he's whining to come up,' objected Jane, dismayed. The hysterical clamour of a Cairn terrier phenomenally separated from his own rose up from below.

'We'd better go down to him,' said John wearily, acknowledging one more victory for silliness. 'Here come the workmen anyway. We'd only be in their way. Here – put your foot *here*, ass.'

They vanished. Insane noises of reunion uprose; then silence. She knew that Jane had made off, her purely subjective frivolous interest exhausted; but that John had taken up his post for the day, a scientific observer with ears of deepening carmine, waiting, under the influence of an inexpressible desire for co-operation, for a chance to steady the ladder, hand up a tool, or otherwise insinuate himself within the framework of the ritual.

Up came the bee man and his mate. They set to work to lift the leads. They communicated with each other in a low drone, bee-like, rising and sinking in a minor key, punctuated by an occasional deep-throated 'Ah!' Knocking, hammering, wrenching developed. Somebody should tell them she could not stand it. Nobody would. She rang for the curtains to be drawn, and when they were, she lay down flat and turned her face to the wall and sank into burning sleep.

She woke to the sound of John shouting through her door.

'They've gone to have their lunch. He's coming back this afternoon to take the swarm. Most of the roof's off. I've seen the bees. If only you'd drawn back your curtains you could have too. I called to you but you didn't seem to hear. The cat's brought in two more birds, a pigeon and a tit, but we saved them and we're thawing them behind the boiler.'

Down the passage he went, stumping and whistling.

Three o'clock. The petrified day had hardened from hour to hour. But as light began to fail, there came a moment when the blue spirit drew closer, explored the treetops, bloomed against the ghostly pane; like a blue tide returning, invading the white caves, the unfructifying salt stones of the sea.

The ladder shook. He was there again, carrying a kind of lamp with a funnel from which poured black smoke. 'Take a look,' he called cheerfully. 'It's worth it. Don't suppose you ever see nothink o' the kind before.'

She rose from her bed, put on dressing-gown and shawl and stumbled to the window. With a showman's flourish he flung off the black sacking – and what a sight was revealed! Atolls of pale honeycomb ridging the length and breadth of beam and lath, thrusting down in serrated blocks into the cavity; the vast amorphous murmuring black swarm suddenly exposed, stirring resentful, helpless, transfixed in the icy air. A few of the more vigorous insects crawled out from the conglomeration, spun up into the air, fell back stupefied.

'They're more lively than you'd think for,' said the bee man, thoughtful. She pointed to his face, upon which three or four bees were languidly creeping. He brushed them off with a chuckle. 'They don't hurt me. Been stung too often. Inoculated like.'

He broke off a piece of honeycomb and held it up. She wished so much to hold it in her hand that she forced herself to push down the window, receiving the air's shock like a blow on the face; and took it from him. Frail, blond, brittle, delicate as coral in construction, weightless as a piece of dried sponge or seaweed.

'Dry, see,' said the bee man. 'You won't get much honey out of here. It's all that wet last summer. If I'd 'a' taken this swarm a year ago, you'd a' got a whole heap. You won't get anythink to speak of out of here now.'

She saw now: the papery transparent aspect of these ethereal growths meant a world extinct. She shivered violently, her spirit overwhelmed by symbols of frustration. Her dream had been rich: of honey pouring bountifully out from beneath her roof tree, to be stored up in family jars, in pots and bowls, to spread on the bread and sweeten the puddings, and save herself a little longer from having to tell the children: No more sugar.

Too late! The sweet cheat gone.

'It's no weather to take a swarm,' repeated the bee man. Dejectedly he waved the lamp over the bubbling glistening clumps, giving them a casual smoke-over. 'Still, you wanted the job done.'

She wished to justify herself, to explain the necessity of dis-possessing the bees, to say that she had been waiting for him since September; but she was dumb. She pushed up the window, put the honeycomb on her dressing-table, and tumbled heavily into bed again.

Her Enemy, so attentive since the outbreak of the war, whis-pered in her ear:

'Just as I thought. Another sentimental illusion. Schemes to produce food by magic strokes of fortune. Life doesn't arrange stories with happy endings any more, see? *Never again*. This source of energy whose living voice comforted you at dawn, at dusk, saying: We work for you. Our surplus is yours, there for the taking – vanished! You left it to accumulate, thinking: There's time; thinking: when I will. You left it too late. What you took for the hum of growth and plenty is nothing, you see, but the buzz of an outworn machine running down. The workers have eaten up their fruits, there's nothing left for you. It's no use this time, my girl! Supplies are getting scarce for people like you. An end, soon, of getting more than their fair share for dwellers in country houses. Ripe gifts unearned out of traditional walls, no more. All the while your roof was being sealed up patiently, cunningly, with spreading plasters and waxy shrouds.'

Through half-closed eyes she watched him bending, peering here and there. Suddenly he whipped out his knife, plunging his arm forward out of sight. A pause; then up came knife, hand again, lifting a clot of thick yellow sticky stuff. Honey.

'Honey!'

There it was, the richness, the substance. The knife carried a packed edge of crusted sugar, and as he held it up, the syrup began to drip down slow, gummy, amber-dark. Isled in the full attack of total winter there it hung, inviolable, a microcosm of summer, melting in sweet oils.

'Honey!' yelled John from below.

'Now we're all right,' called back the bee man in a happy voice, as if released all at once from his own weight of disappointment. 'Plenty here – right in the corner. Did you ever see anythink so artful? Near shave me not spotting it. Oh, we'll get you some! Run and beg us a dish off Cook, Sonny, and I'll dish you out a nice little lot for your tea.'

She heard the urgency of the start of her son's boots. It was as if he ran away with her, ran through her, bursting all obstacles to be back with the dish before he had gone, to offer it where it was required: his part in the serious task. This pure goodwill and disinterestedness of children, this concentration of spirit so entire that they seemed to fuse with and become the object, lifted her on a cool wave above her sickness, threw her up in a moment of absolute peace, as after love or childbirth, upon a white and abstract shore.

'That's a nice boy you've got,' said the bee man, cutting, scraping busily. 'Sensible. I'm ever so glad to see this honey. There's one thing I do hate to see, and that's a swarm starved.'

The words shocked her. Crawling death by infinitesimal stages. Not a question of no surplus, but of the bare necessities of life. Not making enough to live on. A whole community entombed, like miners trapped.

A scuffle below. John's fluting voice came up:

'This do?'

'Fine. Bring it up, Sonny.'

The largest meat platter from the kitchen dresser hove in sight.

'Thanks, mate. Now we'll get you a bit o' somethink to sweeten you. Need it? What does your Mammy think, eh?' He shouted with laughter.

Unable to cope with repartee of so personal a character, John cast her a wry self-conscious grin, and rapidly vanished.

Light was rapidly failing, but the rising moon arrested the descent of darkness. In the opaque bleached twilight his silhouette persisted on the pane, bending, straightening. He hummed and whistled. Now and then he spoke softly to the bees. 'Run off, my girl, run off.' Once he held up his hands to show her the insects clustering upon them.

'They don't worry me, the jokers. Just a sore sort of a tingle, like as if I'd rapped myself over the fingers with a hammer.'

He brushed them off and they fell down like a string of beads breaking. They smiled at one another. She closed her eyes.

Roused by a rap on the pane, she lay in confused alarm. The lower window ran up with a swift screech, and, heaving towards her over the sill in the semi-darkness, she saw a phantasmagoric figure climb in and straighten itself up. A headless figure. Where the face should have been, nothing but swaying darkness. It's the fever. Wait, and it will go away.

She found courage to switch on the lamp and saw the bee man. He was wearing a round hat with a long circular veil of thick gauze that hung to his shoulders.

Fishing up a fragment of voice she croaked:

'Is that your hat for taking swarms?'

'Oh, him,' he said laughing, removing it. 'Forgot I had him on. Did I give you a scare?'

'Stylish,' she said.

'Thought you'd like to know the job's done. I've got 'em down below there. Got you a nice bit of honey, too. I'm glad of that. I hate to see a swarm starved.'

He drew her curtains together. 'Better dror 'em or you'll get into trouble with the black-out, bother it.' Then he moved over to the fireplace. 'Your fire's gorn right down. That's why I come in. Thought I'd make it up for you.' He knelt down, riddled the ashes, and with his bruised, swollen, wax-stuck fingers piled on more coal. 'That'll be more cheerful soon. Ain't you got nobody to see to you then?'

'Oh, yes,' she whispered. 'There'll be somebody coming soon. I forgot to ring.' She felt self-pity, and wanted to weep.

'You do seem poorly. You need giving your chest a good rub with camphorated. I believe in that.'

In another few moments he would be rubbing her chest.

But he remained by the fire, looking thoughtfully round the room. 'This is a nice old place. I knew it when I was a young lad, of course. The old Squire used to have us up for evening classes. Improve our minds. He was a great one for that.' He chuckled. 'Must be ten years since he died. I'm out o' touch. Went out to Canada when I was seventeen. Twenty years ago that was. Never got a wife, nor a fortune, nor nothink.' He chuckled again. 'I'm glad I got back before this war. Back where I started – that's where I am. Living with my married sister.'

She said:

'Won't you have a cup of tea?'

'No, I'll be off home, thanks all the same. I'd best get that swarm in. They're in a bad way.'

'Will they recover?'

'Ah, I couldn't say. It wasn't no weather to take a swarm. And then it demoralises 'em like when you steals their honey. They sings a mournful song – ever so mournful.' He strode to the window. 'Still, we'll hope for the best. George'll be up in the morning to put them leads right. Well, I'll wish you good-night. Hope you'll be more yourself to-morrow.' At the window he paused. 'Well, there's no call to go out that way, is there?' he remarked. 'Might as well go out like a Christian.'

He marched briskly across the room, opened her bedroom door, closed it quietly after him. She heard his light feet on the oak staircase, dying away.

She took her temperature and found it was lower: barely a hundred. He had done her good. Then she lay listening to the silence she had created. One performs acts of will, and in doing so one commits acts of negation and destruction. A portion of life is suppressed for ever. The image of the ruined balcony weighed upon her: torn out, exposed, violated, obscene as the photograph of a bombed house.

What an extraordinary day, what an odd meeting and parting. It seemed to her that her passive, dreaming, leisured life was nothing, in the last analysis, but a fluid element for receiving and preserving faint paradoxical images and symbols. They were all she ultimately remembered.

Somewhere in the garden a big branch snapped off and fell crackling down.

The children burst in, carrying plates of honey.

'Want some?'

'Not now, thanks. I can't really swallow anything, not even delicious honey.'

'It isn't delicious. It's beastly. It looks like seccotine[10] and it tastes *much* too sweet. Ugh!'

It was certainly an unappetising colour – almost brown; the texture gluey. It had been there too long. She croaked:

'You oughtn't to be in this room. Where's Mary? Don't come near me.'

'Oh, we shan't catch your old 'flu,' said John, throwing himself negligently backwards over the arm of the sofa and writhing on the floor. 'Look here, Mum, what on earth did you want to get rid of the poor blighters for? They never did any harm.'

'Think what a maddening noise they made.'

'We like the noise. If you can't stand the hum of a wretched little bee, what'll you do in an air-raid?'

'You had a lovely day watching the bee man.'

'I dare say.'

But now all was loss, satiety, disappointment.

'Think how everybody got stung last summer. Poor Robert. And Mr. Fanshawe.'

'Oh, your old visitors.'

What an entertainment the bees had been, a topic, a focusing point at week-ends. But from now on, of course, there would be no more week-end parties. It was time for the bees to go.

'Remember Jane's eye, all bandaged up for days.'

'I remember that.' Jane flushed, went solemn. 'It didn't 'alf 'urt.'

'Your *English*!' cried John, revolted.

'I got not 'alf off Pippy Didcock,' said Jane, complacent. 'They all says that. It's Oxfordshire accident.'

She started to run up and down the room, kilt flying, hair bouncing, then stood still, her hand on her chest.

'What's the most important thing about a person?' she said.

'Dopey,' said her brother. 'What's biting you?'

'Don't you know?' said Jane. 'Your heart. If it stops, you die. I can hear mine after that running.'

'It won't stop,' said her mother.

'It will some day,' said John. 'It might stop to-night. Reminds me –' He fished in his pocket and drew out a dark object. 'I brought up this tit to give it a last chance by your fire. It was at the back of the boiler, but the cats would keep prowling about. They got the pigeon. It must have been stiff eating.' He examined the tit. 'It's alive!'

He rushed with it to the fire and crouched down, holding it in his palms before the now leaping flames. 'Its eyes opened. It's fluttering.'

Jane came and knelt beside him.

'Isn't it a *sweet* little tiny bird?'

Suddenly it flew straight up out of his hands, dashed against the mantelpiece, fell down again upon the hearthrug. They were all perfectly silent.

After a moment his hand went out to pick it up again. Then it flew straight into the fire, and started to roast, to whitt and cheep over the coals.

In a split second she was there, plunged in her hand, out again. Smell of burnt feathers, charred fragments flaking down. It was on the hearth-stone. Everybody stared.

Suddenly it revived, it began to stagger about. The tenacity of life in its minute frame appalled her. Over the carpet it bounced, one wing burnt off, one leg shrivelled up under its breast, no tail; up and down, vigorously, round and about.

'Is it going to be alive?' said Jane.

'Yes,' said John coldly, heavily. 'We can't do anything about it now.'

Wonderful Holidays

I

At 10:30 p.m. the telephone rang. John's voice came through, more than usually clipped.

'Look here, Mummy, I can't get back to-night.'

He had been absent since morning at the Carmichaels', a quarter of a mile away, and had rung up at intervals throughout the day to announce ineluctable non-return. Business, not pleasure, was detaining him. He and the Carmichael boys were getting the whole programme for the theatricals fixed once and for all. They were going to sketch out a topical revue, throw it roughly into shape, make a final list of properties, rig up a microphone and construct an electric bell.

'Can't get back?'

'Not possibly.'

Duty, said the voice, is paramount. No need, I presume, to point that out? Standing in the unlit hall, she saw her own image glide out before her into the future in multiple projection: a far-flung monotonously repeated line of her, fixed in a puppet's pathos and ignominy, over and over again lifting the instrument to her ear to receive similar announcements.

'What's happened?'

'Well, I've got to turn the horse.'

'Turn the what?'

'Turn the horse. Gerald's horse – Conker.'

'Why must Conker be turned?'

'He's got colic. The vet. says there's a hundred to one chance for him if he's turned every four hours.'

'Couldn't Gerald turn him?'

'Single-handed?' inquired the voice, sick of foolishness. 'He's lying down. It takes four to turn him. We've just done it – me, Gerald, Oliver and Roger Wickham – the chap who's staying. Gerald proposes to set his alarm clock for two a.m. and six, and wake me, and honestly it only means ten minutes out of bed, and I'll sleep like a top in between.'

'Has your hostess been consulted?'

'Of course. There's a bed for me; and as a matter of fact she said she'd be frightfully grateful for my help, because otherwise Mr. Carmichael will have to be roused up, and she's not awfully keen to suggest it to him. But she said I must ask you first if you O.K.d it.'

'That's all right. Only swear you won't go out with no clothes on.'

'I swear.' Immediately his voice relaxed, eager, filial obedience itself. 'As a matter of fact, I shan't bother to undress at all.'

'I hope Conker pulls through.'

'Thanks awfully. Look, don't worry about the show. We're getting on fine with everything. We've roughed out our own thing and we'll polish it off in no time now. Jane and Meg's thing is coming along fine. They're nearly word perfect already: we put them through their parts this afternoon. Roger's been doing his imitations. They're wizard. He and Gerald and Oliver are going to put on an impromptu turn, with him at the piano. That can run to absolutely any length, so you needn't worry about the programme being too short.'

'I don't worry about that. I only worry about there being no programme at all. Only five days, you know.'

'Oh, it'll work out O.K. Roger knows a chap who plays the accordion who might consent to come at a pinch. Daly – he's in the eleven. And Mrs. Carmichael's on the track of a conjurer, though I can't myself see it's necessary. And then there's your thing. How've you been getting on?'

'I haven't learnt my part yet. I've been doing the ironing.'

'Oh, well, you can have a go at it in bed.'

'Has Mrs. Carmichael learnt her part?'

'Not yet. She's having rather bad luck with the animals, as a matter of fact. Not only Conker. Bertha's been giving milk the wrong colour all day.'

'What colour has it been?'

'Well, Mrs. Wilfer, that's her new cook who came yesterday, says it's green and she won't give it to her baby any more. She says it's upset it. So the vet.'s taken away a sample to test. Mr. Carmichael says it's all rot, and we think so too, but Mrs. Carmichael says the more she stares at it the more it seems to take on a sort of greenish tinge; and what with that and the house being full she can't concentrate on her part. She told me to give you her love and say she could rehearse with you to-morrow morning.'

'I can't. I've got to bicycle to Redbury and hunt for Jane's trunk. Give her my love and say could she manage the after-noon.'

'I doubt if she can from what she said, but I'll ask. Well, good-night.'

'Night night. See you for breakfast, I suppose. Have a good time.'

'Rather. Good-night.'

The moment she had rung up, Jane's voice arose on a full horn-like note from a point above the ceiling.

'Who was that?'

'Why aren't you asleep? It was John. He's staying the night at the Carmichaels.'

'Why is he?'

She yelled up the stairs, explaining why.

'Oh, *can't* I help turn him, too? Ring up again and ask. Is Meg going to?'

'I'm sure Meg's asleep hours ago.'

'I bet she's not. I bet she isn't even in bed yet. She told me Gerald and Oliver always beg for her to stay up and she's allowed. She never goes to bed till twelve, she said so. Ring up and ask if I can sleep on the sofa in her room. I could get dressed in five minutes and run along the lane. It's moonlight.'

'No, you can't.'

'John has all the excitements. I'm much more fond of horses than him.'

'Go to sleep, Jane.'

'Do you think Conker'll die?'

'I don't know, I'm sure. I'm afraid he might.'

'You don't sound as if you cared. Poor Conker!'

Silence.

'If he dies, how will they bury him?'

'I don't know. I haven't thought.'

'Do horses have graveyards?'

'No, they don't have graveyards.'

Silence. She sank into the arm-chair, took up a tenuous, worn, paper-bound volume and began to study it. A note in Aunt Cicely's slapdash hand fell out of the pages.

DEAREST M.,

   Your dear M. told me last night on the phone of your difficulties re suitable sketches for your S. the S. Week, and it struck me the encl. found last week in turning out old papers for salvage might help you out??? I remember Aunt G. and I did it many years ago – before we were married, in fact!!! – to raise money for the new organ – and it caused roars of laughter!! Of course the villages are so much more go-ahead nowadays, with all this crooning, etc. (Mrs. H.'s Group is getting up N. Coward for the Comforts Fund in May – aiming TOO high, I think!!??!!) but sometimes these old-fashioned things come up unexp. fresh again – in fact curiously enough Lady P. was telling me y'day her W.I. did it last Xmas and it was considered most amusing, and with your cleverness you could easily bring it up to date – changing bonnets to toques or perhaps better still simply hats?? (Lady P. did this) etc. etc. There is the little difficulty of Miss Brown stating her age as 25?? – not that you look much more than that dear and in any case I ALWAYS took it this was MEANT to raise a laugh. Best of luck dear for the great week. Try not to wear yourself out. If people seem willing they are apt to get put upon at these times and I know what you are. Our own target was £500 and we raised £974!!!! – thanks to Sir W.

– Your loving Aunt C.

You must do it. You can and you will. Only fifteen minutes out of a lifetime, and you'll feel so happy afterwards. Think what women are doing nowadays... If it went down with Lady P.'s W.I., why shouldn't it go down here? They're not so very critical...? *Forget yourself* – that's the thing – clown away for all you're worth, make the most of the *business*, particularly bringing on the bath. Failing a hip-bath, must make do with the bigger zinc egg-bucket, but of course not so humorous. *Must not* dry up – that's the chief thing. If you're word perfect you get the confidence to go for the comedy... Will Mrs. Carmichael not dry up...?

Once more the horn sounded from above, firm, melancholic.

'Come up.'

She went up. Invisible, Jane stirred in her bed.

'I saw a shop in Redbury. It said, "Horse meat. Not for human consumption." What does that mean?'

'It means for animals – dogs and cats.'

'I see. Might a kind of horse like Conker go there?'

'No, I promise you.'

'Good. I wish there wasn't any meat in the world. Meat, meat, nothing but meat.'

'Not much nowadays.'

'There oughtn't to be one single scrap. Oh, it's beastly! How do we know sheep and calves and all that don't want to have their lives as much as we do?'

'Who always asks if it can't be stew for lunch?'

'It's not my favourite. It never was. I can't stand such a world.' She thrashed about between the sheets.

'Oh, darling, don't let's start that again. I can't do anything about it.'

The silence swelled with immensities of moral conflict and indictment. She stood, accused, by the bed in the dark, and heard the rhythmical throat of night begin to throb and croon again. Bomb, bomb, bomb, bomb. Burn, burn, burn, burn. Down, down, down, down. Fuller, fuller, fainter, fainter. A strong force of our aircraft passing overhead. Impersonally exulting and lamenting, deadly mild, soothing in its husky reiterated burden as a familiar lullaby. Four years safe beneath this portion of the unimpartial sky, Jane, who had called out on the first night of war: 'Do they make special small bombs for children?' heard it now without listening; feared only the unpropitiated presence of the night wind knocking and writhing in the curtain.

'Think of sleepy things.'

She was aware of Jane's eyes closing in instant automatic response.

'Say them.'

She said them.

'Yes, and what else?'

'Think of all the lovely things to look forward to.'

'What are they?'

'The theatricals. Acting for the first time with the big ones and going to Mrs. Carmichael's party afterwards. Staying up till midnight, I should think. Daphne coming on Wednesday to stay.'

'I shall think about Roger. Honestly, Mummy, he's the wittiest boy I've ever met. Oh, he's wonderful! He keeps such a grave face, and all the time he's saying funny things. He catches me out with them, because they're witty. Oh, he makes me and Meg laugh so! Meg understands them, because she's got a sense of humour. I wish I had. Do you think I shall ever get one? How can I?'

'Perhaps you'll grow one. People often do after they're ten.'

'John says I never shall. Roger's going to paint our portraits, Meg and me together. Honestly, he's a simply wonderful painter. But what am I to wear? I *cannot* be painted in my dirty uniform. I got a lot more spots on it to-day. John says it makes my face the colour of a cooked mushroom. What am I to do?'

'I can't think. I'm just praying your trunk will turn up to-morrow.'

'God, God, I hope so!'

'I'm going to the station directly after breakfast. It's no use keeping on telephoning all over the place. I believe it might be sitting at the station all the time, in a siding or something, with the label torn off.'

The school trunk, sent in advance at the end of the term, had failed to arrive. For ten days Jane, in alternating moods of protest, resignation, complacence or mere indifference, had bicycled, climbed, ridden Meg's pony, gone out to tea, clad in the Sunday uniform frock, once palest hospital grey, in which she had been despatched from school.

'Honestly, I cannot wear it one day longer. I'm sick and tired of the filth of it. It doesn't suit me, anyway. John's always tweaking it and saying: "What ho! for a public schoolgirl," and things like that. I'm sure Roger hates it… though he says grey's one of his favourite colours.'

'If I don't have any luck to-morrow, I'll ask Mrs. Carmichael if she could possibly lend you something of Meg's.'

'Meg's things are all too tight. *Oh dear!* Aren't the Carmichaels lucky to have Roger staying?'

'Extremely lucky.'

'Which do you like the best: Gerald, Oliver or Roger?'

'I like them all.'

'All exactly the same? I did like Oliver best… And Gerald's very nice… But I'm not so sure now,' She faintly groaned.

'I believe you'll be asleep in exactly one minute. Goodnight, pet.' Their faces bumped in the dark. Jane's cool arms clasped her neck in a stranglehold, then fell away.

'Oh, you beauty! Stand in the window and let me see you by moonlight.'

'Nonsensical creature. Close your eyes.'

'You know that new leaf I turned over on Easter Day?'

'Yes. How's it getting on?'

'Well, what do you think?'

She racked her brains.

'I supposed you never noticed,' said Jane, invisibly shrugging.

'What?'

'Only I dug a quarter of the bed by the hen-house for you with the big fork: I could manage it.'

'Do you mean it was you?' she exclaimed, disingenuous. 'I noticed it to-night when I went to shut up the hens. I thought Old Arthur must have started on it for the potatoes.'

'I sincerely trust I keep it up. I'll do some more tomorrow; at least, if I have time. It depends how long Roger wants me for. By the way, my stockings have got two new holes. Could you possibly darn them to-night?'

She went downstairs, brought her sewing basket to the fire, sat down and began to darn. Began once more to think about the trunk. Lost. Stolen. Strayed. Strayed. Stolen. Lost. The needle pointed in – blank – out – blank – drawing after it the long grey strand of frustration.

She finished the stocking and started on John's socks. The bellow of glider-towing Whitleys practising night landings half a mile away reverberated round the roof. Just after midnight she finished the last of the socks, extinguished the light, and looked out of the window. The released gliders were tipping, sliding steep down the lustrous sky, one after another: giant pendants set with white, rose and emerald brilliants. Through the roar another sound began to wind and waver: singing. It came from the direction of the Carmichaels': the Eton Boating Song flung without inhibition on the night by a chorus of unmusical and partially immature male voices. It seemed to be going up the lane towards the village.

* * *

John turned up about nine o'clock next morning, unusually fresh and clear-eyed. He had had, he said, an excellent night.

'We thought we might as well stay up till the two o'clock turning,' he said. 'Then we went to bed. Gerald set his alarm for six, but he went out to look at Conker before waking us, and it was just as he thought. So he didn't wake us.'

'Why not?' said Jane.

'Conker had croaked,' said John, attacking porridge.

'*Croaked?*'

'Dead.'

Jane stopped in the act of mastication. Her throat closed, slowly her face grew bursting, darkly red.

'Oh, well,' said John, 'he was twenty-five at least.'

Jane swallowed with an effort.

'What are they going to do with him?' she said, low.

'They've rung up the kennels,' said John off-hand.

'The what?'

'What was that caterwauling about midnight last night?' she interposed swiftly, grimacing at him over Jane's bowed head. 'It sounded like the Eton Boating Song rendered by maniacs. Could it have been an hallucination?'

'No,' said John, faintly grinning. 'It was us. We got appallingly hungry working so late, and the larder got pretty well bare, so we had to buzz up to Mr. MacBean for more dough cakes. We stayed around in the bakehouse for a bit and gave him a hand.'

'Was he pleased to see you?'

'Rather. Why not? It must be pretty boring alone there at night. We helped him shove the loaves into the oven.' She saw them bursting at dead of night into the warm, bright aromatic bakehouse, their idle elastic limbs at large among the materials and gear of production, their brilliant tumbling locks and smooth wax-mask faces revolving in light-hearted irresponsibility around the bald, intellectual dome, the spectacled transparent face moulded in hollows and lines of sensibility, humour and exhaustion, the swiftly kneading hands of dear Mr. MacBean. He delivered the milk before breakfast, served all day in the store, teasing and wisecracking with his customers, made bread each night into the small hours, and only snapped in gusts of blind scorching rage when it came to the stock-taking or the forms, or a bother with the booking. 'They're some smart lads,' he would say with a chuckle and shake of his head, when she apologised for the perpetual raids on the dough cakes. 'That age, you got a wolf in your stomach.'

John pushed away his porridge and started to hack at the loaf.

'Go slow with the marmalade. That's the last of it; and another week till the new period.'

'Oh, well… It's no use screwing out these wretched snips and scraps. It's simply training us to have mean natures. By the time we're grown up we'll be crawling round with paper bags picking up crumbs and cheese parings and tea leaves off the floors. How would you like that?' He cut a thick crooked slice, adding: 'I'm not awfully hungry as a matter of fact. I had a whacking breakfast at the Carmichaels'.'

'What did you have?' said Jane, sharp.

The telephone bell rang.

'I'll answer it,' said John, bounding towards it. 'Sure to be Gerald or Oliver about the footlights.'

He took up the receiver, said 'Hallo, yes,' then, 'Hold on please. What name shall I say?'

Pause.

'Who?'

Pause.

'*Who?*' He threw down the receiver, disgusted. 'For you.'

'Who is it?'

'God knows. Some lunatic.'

She took up the receiver and said, 'Hallo.'

A rough voice trumpeted out: ''Morning, Mrs. Ritchie. The Vicar here.'

'Oh, Mr. Jebb! Good-morning. Do forgive my boy. He didn't seem to recognise the word vicar. He's not been very well brought up.'

Harsh nasal giggles rasped her ear.

'That's all right, Mrs. Ritchie. No offence meant, none taken. If you will send your boy to Eton, what can you expect? Hach! Hach! Hach! No offence meant. He seems a decent sort of lad on the whole. But I say, though! – beastly lot they're turning out everywhere to-day – public schools and all. Damned impudent swearing young brutes. All smoking like chimneys. Girls just as bad. If not worse. Vile lot. It's all the fault of the parents. What goes on in the homes nowadays? Nothing but beastly bad language – that's all they hear. What can you expect? It's a filthy outlook. I say, look here, there's another damned nuisance coming on us. Book drive in June, or some such rot. Who ever heard of a book drive? Heard of a whist drive, never heard of a book drive. Suppose these damned official brutes can't find anything better to do than pester us with their tomfoolery. We can't call our souls our own. Personally speaking, can't see we'd be any worse off under the Nazis. I say, I'd be much obliged if you'd come on the committee. You know what's what, I take it, in these matters.'

He continued in bitterness and scorn to explain the scheme.

'All right, Mr. Jebb. I'll do it, with pleasure. Who else will be on the committee?'

'Damned if I know. Thought I'd better tackle Mrs. Venables. She knows what's what, I take it. But she's a bit on the peevish side, eh? – between you and me. Don't know if you hit it off with her. I can't. Filthy tempered woman. Then there's those Miss What-d'you-call-ems – that new lot, taken Flint Cottage – call themselves journalists, don't they? Have you come across them? They've borrowed my roller. Take my advice, steer clear of 'em. Got up like streetwalkers. I suppose they know what's what, but if you ask me, they're not respectable. Then there's Mrs. Jessop – she's up to her eyes. Says her husband's put his foot down – won't let her take on anything more.'

'I wish somebody's foot would come down on me when I'm asked to take on anything more: I do seem to get awfully crushed without it.'

The receiver became totally silent; then started to caw and crackle as if in the grip of an electric storm. Spasm after spasm wheezed through it. He'd seen it, he'd got there. Rich, rich – that's what it was: rich. Never know what the woman will say next.

'Perhaps Mrs. Carmichael would help?' she said when he grew calmer. 'She knows what's what.'

'A bit harum scarum, Mrs. Carmichael. I'm not saying anything against her, but she's a bit of a gad-about. Always on her bicycle – tearing in and out of Redbury. Don't know what she does there.'

'She makes camouflage nets three days a week.'

'Oh, that stuff. Knew she was poking her nose into something. I say! she's not what she was before the war, you know. I rather liked Mrs. Carmichael before the war... There's that old fool Parkinson; he knows what's what – he's a classical man, like me. He'd bite my head off if I asked him to come on the committee. Then there's Mrs. Moffat – she's an obliging sort of woman, but she can't take on anything more.'

'Oh, yes, poor dear, she's had to go to London to nurse her aunt, hasn't she?'

'Yes. Nasty long job – cancer. London's bound to get it in the neck again, too – any moment. But I say! – between you and me, it's the best thing out for Captain Moffat.'

'Do you think so?'

'He's a different man. Hadn't you noticed? Digging in his garden yesterday – quite spry. Squaring his shoulders up. She's too soft with him, you know – coddles him. Makes him look a fool. I said to him yesterday: "I say! Where's your bonnet and shawl? I'll tell your wife on you." Hach! Hach! Hach! This east wind touched you up anywhere? Be in the east now till the end of May. It's touched up my knee again, but I keep on. Got to keep on till we drop. That's what these Beveridge brutes are after, I take it: work us till we drop, then shovel us out and sit on our graves and twiddle their thumbs. I say! What d'you think of the Archbishop?'

'Well... what do *you* think of him, Mr. Jebb?'

'Off his head.' He told her for three minutes what he thought of his Father in God.

'I'm sure you're right. Well, Mr. Jebb, I must –'

'I say! Where's the Luftwoffer? What are they up to with this Second Front?'

He told her for two minutes the strategic dispositions of the Allied generals, the nature of the secret weapon, and of the tactics about to be adopted by the German Air Force. Then he said abruptly: 'Ta-ta, Mrs. Ritchie,' and rang off.

'You encourage him,' said John.

'I do not. I can't discourage him: that's quite another matter. You must learn to be more accurate.'

'Shall you marry him, Mummy?' said Jane.

She danced in a corner of the room, throwing her arms out in free, dreamy gesturings and revolving in her bedroom slippers with a fairly obvious intention of languorous grace.

'No. I'm off now. Unless some clue seems to point me on to Paddington, Bristol or Penzance, I ought to be back about lunch-time.'

'With my trunk?' said Jane.

'Who knows? If you hear a taxi stop outside the door, it'll be me with the trunk. If you hear a bicycle stop, it'll be just me again.'

'Aha! I guess it'll be a taxi. Don't you, Mummy?'

Jane's eyes rolled, illumined with prophetic ecstasy. She tripped across the room, spreading sunshine, flinging up her arms. Her smirched grey-belted front tautened over her expanding stomach.

'Oh, Jane, you look like a hoarding that's been rained on and scrawled over for six weeks. *Why* not wear those old grey flannels of John's and his St. Michael's football jersey?'

'Oh, *no! Not those awful braces again.* I *can't!*'

'What's wrong with them?'

'Well, *don't you see…?* It's that back bit. I have to unbutton them all round and then I can't get at that back bit again, I simply can't catch it to button them on again. So what I have to do is to undress *completely*, to my vest, when I go, every time, and then dress again, and last time at the Carmichaels' when I spent the day I had to go once, and when you come out you get looks as if to say: "You've been a jolly long time." It's not very nice.'

A cracked hoot came sharply out of John. After a few moments he tottered to the arm-chair and collapsed in it, twisting and beating his head about. Dumb convulsions interspersed with gasps and whimpers shook his frame. He lay back on the cushions, his hair on end, eyes closed, face flushed, distorted and said faintly:

'Oh, let me die. Take pity on me, someone. Carry me away.'

'What's the joke?' said Jane, sombre, standing in front of him and pushing his nerveless heels about with her toes. Another spasm clutched him. He checked it with a groan, and murmured, wiping his eyes:

'Why not call on Roger for assistance? He's a helpful sort of chap.'

'SHUT UP!'

Jane hurled herself and fell on him, pounding, clawing, savaging him. This time it would happen: arm-chair, limbs, torsos, heaving, grunting, interlocked, would break up all together and be dismembered on the carpet.

'*Not* in that chair!'

At once their bodies slid to the floor. She went upstairs to tie a scarf round her head, hearing, from below, the violence batter round the room and thin out in familiar, progressive stages. Thuds. Screeches. Threats. Jibes. Giggling and grumbling. Twitters. Silence.

When she came down John was rummaging in his jar of screws and nails, Jane sunk in the current number of *Sunny Stories*. They looked placid and refreshed, starting the day with quiet indoor occupations: an agreeable picture.

'Well, good-bye for the present,' she said. 'Can you reveal your plans? Just so that I don't spend the next few hours in helpless anxiety.'

'I'm starting for the Hall as soon as Oliver telephones,' said John. 'We're going to get the stage up this morning.'

'Meg's coming over here,' said Jane. 'We're going to hear each other our parts and finish the posters. But oh, I need my poster paints that are in my trunk. Oh, my trunk, my darling trunk!

Oh, Mummy, my helpless anxiety! Oh, Mummy, Mummy, promise me to bring it back. Promise your little girl.'

She flung down *Sunny Stories* and floated towards her, arms outstretched in tender yearning.

'Stage this morning. Rehearsal directly after lunch. Footlights after tea. Full day,' said John. He let out a wild snatch of tuneless whistling. 'Where's my screwdriver gone again? What stinking hell-hound –'

The telephone bell rang. Roughly assembling his joints, he corkscrewed thunderously upon the instrument.

'That you? O.K. Starting now.' He was gruff, on the job. A loud gurgling sound as of flood-water bubbling in full spate down gutters cut him off. 'Pipe down, can't you? You tickle –'

'That's Oliver,' breathed Jane, softly radiant. 'Or Gerald.'

She picked up two chairs overthrown in his elliptical swoop and went out of the front door, up the path towards the bicycle shed, followed by Jane. The wind blew from the east, but the sun was brilliant. The thought of skimming downhill between cherry orchards consoled her.

'You needn't feel your tyres,' said Jane. 'I've pumped them up. You didn't know, did you? It's my good deed for the day.'

They hugged and kissed at the shed door, by the waiting bicycle.

'Mind you learn your part and get those posters done.'

'Of course. Roger might want to paint me this morning, though. What then?'

'I suppose you might tell him you've got to learn your part and finish the posters.'

She mounted and wobbled out into the road. After a short delay the yell came after her.

'I couldn't say that!'

She waved without looking back and pedalled on.

Redbury Station was stretched out stiff with emptiness and silence. One boy, holding a notebook and a pencil, stood on the bridge, staring up the line; a tranced and fanatical figure. She tried the door of the parcels office and found it locked. She knocked on the door marked Station Master and put her head in. The young lady booking-office clerk was inside, enjoying a cup of tea with a friend; she said regretfully that she couldn't think wherever Mr. Hobbs could have got to. He'd flagged out the ten forty-two some minutes ago; he must have gone off to see to something; he was bound to be somewhere. It wasn't their busy time just now, but he was sure to be back soon.

She looked along the vacant platform and saw at the far end the form of Mr. Hobbs, in his frock-coat and peaked cap, bending over a mixed bed of tulips and broccoli. When she came up to him he straightened himself and said cordially:

'Ah, it's you. Good-morning. You've come about that there trunk.'

The confident, even triumphant, note in his voice caused a wild hope to shoot through her: the trunk had arrived, was waiting...?

'No, there's nothing come yet. It's a funny thing.'

'It is a funny thing.'

'I've been on the phone to Brading, but they haven't clapped eyes on it. And a wire came from Shippenham this a.m. They sent it off all right on the twenty-fourth, according to that.'

'Oh, they did send it off?'

'Oh, they sent it off all right, no doubt about that.'

'But they can't trace it?'

'Oh, they can't trace it. That's the finish of it for them when they've checked and despatched. If you care to come along, I'll show you what they say.'

She went along beside him.

'This is the twelfth day, Mr. Hobbs. Do you think I should give up hope?'

'Oh, I wouldn't do that. I wouldn't give up 'ope. No need. Not yet. I've known 'em take a month and turn up as cool as cucumbers. I 'ad a lady's bicycle took six months.'

'Things do get stolen quite a lot these days, I suppose?'

'There's that, of course. And then there's the under-staffing. And the mislaying due to ignorance: the ignorance is shocking. But laying all that on the side, there's a lot of funny things occurring on the lines just now. Heavy traffic. Priority. If you take my meaning.'

'I do.' She charged her voice with significant reserve.

'Ah.' His ginger mustache sprang forward, wary, sealing careless talk. 'My boy's 'ad 'is leave stopped. You can fancy what's be'ind that. And what I look at in your little trouble is – it's not known general, but I don't see the 'arm in easing your mind if you keep it to yourself – you aren't the only one to be in a bit of a 'ole, I shouldn't be surprised. From what I 'ear, there was a rare lot of stuff sent off in advance booked passenger that's gone goods these 'olidays. That being the case, you've no call to give up 'ope, not for another three weeks.'

'Three weeks? The summer term starts in less than three weeks.'

He unlocked the door of the parcels office, saying:

'You can take a look round just to satisfy your mind, but we got nothing answering.'

There was nothing in the parcels office except a corded *papier-mâché* suitcase, a child's push-chair, two crates and a sack.

At his suggestion they returned to his office to have another go through the particulars.

'Yes, that's all correct,' she said, depressed.

'Oh, I've got the matter in hand,' he said, bracing. 'You leave it to me. I'll keep on at them. The moment I hear, I'll ring through.'

'What I'm afraid of is,' she confessed, abashed, 'that the labels have got torn off and it's just sitting on some platform between here and Shippenham.'

'Oh, it wouldn't have done that. It wouldn't have got left sat on a platform. It 'ud 'ave got put somewhere pending inquiries and claim. Oh, yes.'

'If it doesn't come by the week-end, I shall start out and ransack every parcels office and every truck in every siding on this line – starting from London.'

At this the young lady clerk and her friend softly clicked their tongue, marking a sympathetic sense of desperation. She looked towards them, careworn, uncomplaining, and said:

'Exactly what she stands up in. Not another stitch.'

'Ah, they do grow,' said the friend, a matron. 'It's a job these days.'

'It's a shame,' said the young lady, single, but a mother type.

'I've washed her underclothes out twice and dried them overnight.'

'Ah, and you don't like to do that too often,' said the young lady.

'Pore little soul, bless 'er,' said the friend.

They were so kind, so compassionate, she could have cried. They knew how it was.

'She's got all her own belongings packed in it – that's what's worrying her. Her teddy-bear and books and paint-box... You know.'

'All her little treasures,' said the friend.

'A trunk means such a lot to a child,' said the young lady.

'Ah, it's the sentimental value,' agreed Mr. Hobbs, a family man himself. He opened a drawer of his table and turned up some papers. 'There'd be no 'arm in filling out a form to go on with. You can always claim against the company for loss, you know. Here you are. It's all put out clear, see: state your items down this column, value of each – approximate to what you consider right – alongside each, down 'ere.'

With a further sinking of spirits she took the paper. He knew, then, in his heart of hearts, that it was lost. All that optimism was so much bluff to get rid of her. She said bitterly:

'What about coupons?'

'That's where it is,' said the friend.

'Ah, that would be a separate form.' He scratched his head. 'That 'ud be more the Board of Trade, I fancy. I don't rightly know what they'd say to a claim of this sort of a nature. There's no 'arm in trying.'

'It's not so much the finance,' crooned the young lady.

'It's the kewpons.'

'And when you get the kewpons,' said the friend, 'you can't get the value. *Shoes*…! It is a job.'

'Well, Mr. Hobbs, thank you for all you've done. I won't bother you any longer.'

'Oh, that's all right. You leave it all to me,' he repeated, still patient, but bored now, a little mechanical.

A notion struck her.

'There isn't more than one Redbury, I suppose, is there?'

'More than one Redbury? Oh, yes, there's more than one Redbury. There's Redbury-on-Sea for one.'

'It couldn't have gone there, could it?'

'Well, I don't say it couldn't 'ave done.' Nag, nag, nag: these women. 'That's the Southern, of course. Tell you what I'll do for you: I'll send off a wire there, just on the chance. That's what I'll do. But, mind you, I wouldn't be surprised to see it turning up this morning – or this afternoon, it might do. I wouldn't be at all surprised. I'll give you a ring if it should do.'

So don't keep on with your blessed phone calls... She smiled bravely, wistfully, at them all and went away. Pedalling with urgency, she reached the fishmonger's in time to get the last of the fish: a wedge of glutinous marine flesh, unidentified. Then to Bobbie's Parlour for a cup of coffee essence. With sugar? Please, with sugar. Just a few grains. She lingered, smoking a cigarette. The road climbed uphill all the way.

A fearful compulsion began to grip her. Suppose, only suppose, one went back to the station... Suppose one looked over the bridge and saw on the platform one solitary grey fabric leather-bound trunk, dropped out by the twelve-four, waiting to be claimed? Suppose, on the other hand, the platform perfectly bare, Mr. Hobbs emerged that moment from his office, looking up to catch one insanely peeping?... But then one could simply move on with unflurried dignity, as if after a little rest... Back, back to the station.

She stopped on the bridge and looked down, and it was just as she had dreamed it. There, on the sunlit enchanted platform, one large solitary object, a trunk, a grey school trunk. Mine! Not mine! *Mine!* Nonsense. Calm now. Go forward decorously. It's only another false dawn. Prepare yourself.

When she reached the platform a porter with a barrow was bending over the object, examining the labels. She came on.

'It's mine,' she said without emotion. Her knees trembled.

'That the missing one? Well, I never! I took it off of the twelve-four myself. There you are, then. It's your lucky day. That's the end of your little troubles.'

It looked so beautiful, all in order; no damage, no defacement, the labels correctly addressed in a clear round hand.

'You'll tell Mr. Hobbs, won't you?'

'Oh, ah, I'll tell 'im. 'E's gorn to 'is lunch just now. What d'you want done with it?' He heaved it on to the barrow.

'I must dash across to Mr. Turnbull and see if he can take me up.'

Walking beside him, she said, suddenly hysterical:

'You don't know what this means to me.'

'Ah, I dare say.'

Only a little while and she would be back home amid triumph and rejoicing. Jane would be in shorts and blue pullover, the grey ruin bundled off to the cleaners, the contents of her linen bag in the suds, the stamp collection pounced on, the specimens of handwork destined for Easter gifts distributed, the poster paints unscrewed; all the possessions reunited with their owner, the diminished personality knit up again, intact.

Everything began to work together for good. As they emerged into the station yard, Mr. Turnbull drove up. It was her lucky day, he said. He'd got a funeral to meet on the one-seventeen, but he'd come along early for a quiet smoke and a read of the papers: seeing it was a special occasion, he didn't mind obliging. They could do it with a sprint.

There was no rapturous bursting open of the door when they stopped before it. Mr. Turnbull, chatty, unloaded trunk and bicycle, dragged the former into the hall and drove away. She called. The house was silent, deserted. Mrs. Plumley came in by the garden door from giving the hens their green stuff, and told her that the children were at the Carmichaels'. They had been in and out, the whole lot of them, all the morning. They had come back round about twelve and left a message: they were stopping for lunch at the Carmichaels', so as to get right on with their rehearsing. They had taken the tin of minced beef and cereal loaf to help out.

Deprived of eleven points' worth of near-meat, she and Mrs. Plumley agreed upon a fried egg each – and bacon? – yes, just a couple of the rashers – and ate them in the kitchen, enjoying the quiet *tete-à-tete* and exchanging the morning's news. The broody hen had entered upon her period of progenitive ritual and retreat in a secluded coop at the bottom of the garden. The other hens had laid to capacity by midday. Judging by her size, appetite, and the spiteful expression on her face, Fluffy had gone and fallen for another lot. It would be that old Ginger from the farm again: Fluffy seemed as if she couldn't resist him.

Old Arthur had put in half of the potatoes and then, feeling a bit knocked up, turned it in for the day. What might be the chances of his coming back to finish them to-morrow? Mrs. Plumley had put that to him; but old Arthur couldn't rightly say. It all depended on what he felt like to-morrow.

It came to light that Mrs. Plumley and Mr. Hobbs had been boy and girl together at Redbury School a fair long time ago. Mrs. Plumley could remember when his mother, old Lizzie Hobbs that was, was taken off to the asylum, singing hymns at the top of her lungs. You had to laugh. It was the change, of course, and a lot of worry on the top of it. In view of this reminiscence, and of other dramas, recollected now in detail, in the life histories of Mr. Hobbs's brothers, sisters and more distant relatives, to dwell on the profundities of emotion caused by a piece of luggage lost and found seemed – though Mrs. Plumley accorded them their due – disproportionate and self-indulgent. Scratch Mr. Hobbs below the surface and you found a being beset by the Eumenides,[11] emerged from strangling mazes to be the man he was. Crippled in the beginnings by family disasters and disgraces, Willie Hobbs had gone steadily forward to win scholarships and do himself credit, to attain his place, his insignia of office, his serene and authoritative pacing of Redbury platform.

Not the Hobbses alone, but all the innumerable specimens impaled beneath Mrs. Plumley's microscopic eye of memory, had been similarly beset. The birth-beds, the death-beds; and in between the schooling, the church, the chapel; the start in life, the rise, the stumble, the downfall: all followed the same banal yet portentous pattern; all were impregnated with the same citric essence of destiny. What accidents, what sickness, what curses, what omens; what eccentricities of pride and humiliation; what diabolical houndings, what selfless generosities; what morbid moral scruples, what coarse jests shrewdly savoured… What impoverishments of speech or total inarticulacies; yet when they spoke out, in their times of joy or doom, they spoke, through Mrs. Plumley's reminiscent lips, with piercing accuracy and an austere majesty of rhythm.

Had Jane and Meg got those posters done, by any chance? Mrs. Plumley thought not; but they were thoroughly enjoying themselves, no doubt of that. Jane's laugh had been ringing out, such a merry peal, enough to cheer you up for the day. As for John, he seemed to be taken real helpless: stretched out on the floor, groaning, when she'd popped her head in. They'd been having a go at their rehearsing, she supposed: there was those young Carmichaels banging on the piano, and that young Mr. Wickham quavering out as grave as a judge: one of those music-hall turns she fancied they were getting up – the two of them aiming to render something sentimental in the way of a duet, and the other one chiming in all wrong every time accidentally on purpose to spoil the effect like.

He did have a way with him, that young Mr. Wickham: you couldn't help but take to him. It wasn't what he said – he was on the quiet side in fact compared to the others – it was the way he said it. Every time he opened his mouth he set you off. She'd been busy down there making the old broody a bit more comfortable, and he'd come tiptoeing up with Jane to have a peep at her. And, oh, lord! if he didn't start crouching down and stretching himself up behind the coop, and flickering with his eyelids, and muttering out some double-dutch as if it was a prayer, and raising his arms up to heaven and fluttering them around. Jane's face was a study. Then he turns, and: 'There, Mrs. Plumley,' he says, very solemn, 'I've seen to it this magnificent hen of yours won't have no disappointments this time. These simple little rites you have just witnessed will guarantee her not only her whole brood of little ones, but very possibly twins out of each egg.' And Jane, opening her big eyes at him as if to say could he mean it... At the recollection, Mrs. Plumley bowed double and rocked like a poplar in a gale. You could see, she added, he was a boy who'd had a nice home and a good bringing-up. He'd make a nice friend for the children. He'd taken a fancy to Jane, you could see that.

'Do you really think so, Mrs. Plumley?' She felt gratified. 'I thought perhaps it was more the other way round.'

But no, said Mrs. Plumley, clinching her point: Jane had gone trotting along down the road with him, swinging on his arm, prattling away, looking up at him so sparkling and roguish, it was a picture.

Wondering with what downward looks he had countered these upward looks, debating the comparative values of inhibition and lack of inhibition in childhood, she helped Mrs. Plumley to wash up.

The telephone bell rang. An official masculine voice enquired with curt nasal sleekness for Mrs. Ritchie.

'Speaking.'

'Films division, M. of I., Brading, here. You were expecting a call from us, I think.'

'Oh, yes, I was. About the films for Saturday. I do hope it's all right?'

'You may remember we told you on the occasion of your visit to us a fortnight ago that we were quite unable to give you a definite promise?'

'Well, yes – only you said you'd do your best, and as I hadn't heard, I sort of assumed –'

'We always do our best, Mrs. Ritchie. We're a Government service, and it's our job to send our shows – free – wherever and whenever the public requires them.'

'Oh, I *know*. The last one you sent was so popular.' And the young operator and the girl friend he brought with him on the van so dashing and agreeable. 'I do so hope you're going to be able to manage Saturday? You know it's to start off our Salute the Soldier week, and the village is simply counting on it. It's advertised and everything.'

'Well, I'm sorry to hear it, Mrs. Ritchie, because we've got a disappointment for you.'

'Have you really?'

'Circumstances over which we have no control.' His voice sharpened to a knife-edge of confidential reticence. 'I dare say you take my meaning.'

'Yes; yes, of course, mm hmm.' Automatically her voice assumed the correct note: knowing but shuttered, unquestioning.

'Three-quarters of our vans gone... Unknown destinations. Simply vanished – so far as the public is concerned, that is. I needn't say more, need I?'

'Oh, no.' I, too, obscure countrywoman, parent and house-wife, am linked with the outer fringes of Authority. Gratifying.

'Consequence is, we've no option but to cut our services to the civilian population. The only van at our disposal Saturday is booked for a show the other side of the county. We've worked out that getting to you would mean a run of fifty miles. Under the circumstances we don't feel justified in such an expenditure of petrol. I'm sure you'll understand.'

'I understand.' She directed a heavy groaning sigh into the mouthpiece. There was no response. 'Well, thank you for letting me know. I'll just have to explain to the village what's happened.'

'I beg your pardon, Mrs. Ritchie?' Voice of shocked alarm.

'I'll just have to write something up on the posters.'

He cleared his throat.

'I don't need to ask *you*, I'm sure, to watch out what – to exercise the utmost discretion in anything you write up.'

'Well, perhaps I won't put the exact invasion date.' Silence. Not amused. 'Perhaps there'd be no harm in writing: "*Unavoidably cancelled*"?'

'Well, I dare say there'd be no harm in that. But the less said the better, you know.'

'*Oh!...*' she broke out, hysteria climbing again within her, 'I shall give up the whole bloody business. *Everything's* gone wrong.'

With a repressive good-bye, he dismissed her and rang off.

She turned from the telephone and saw with a start that a motionless male figure blocked the glass door into the garden. Stiff, melancholy, it stared through a pane and held something on a plate. A raw chop.

'Oh, Captain Moffat!' She flung open the door.

'Awfully sorry to disturb you.' He thrust the plate towards her. 'Could you tell me what I ought to do with this?'

'A chop.' Together they gazed at it, as if unable to believe their eyes.

He muttered far back in his throat, scarcely moving a muscle of his face: 'My wife fixed up with that Higgs girl, Violet, the one who has fits, to come in and see to my meals. But she hasn't turned up to-day. Her mother's just sent down a note which seems to say she's got a swollen face. I found this chop in the larder. I suppose it ought to be cooked. Pity to waste it.' His dry lips closed again, in a dead line. He looked at her intently out of two tiny black pits, extinct.

'What a *shame*!' All feminine sympathy, she beamed on him; then ventured a cheerful laugh. 'It's the most pathetic story I ever heard. What *would* your wife say?'

'She'd take the next train home. She's ringing up tonight to find out how I'm getting on. I shall have to put a good face on it. Can't possibly let her know.' His voice went weak with self-pity.

'No, you couldn't possibly, could you?' she said, gently bracing and threatening. 'She's got enough to worry her, hasn't she?'

He'd let her know all right: trust him. She took the plate from him. 'What a beautiful chop. Now, let me think a minute.'

He stood before her, in sterile resistance, sterile surrender, his arms hanging down by his sides. His will, that beak of brass, lifted above her, guarding him, attacking her.

'I tell you what, Captain Moffat: I'll cook it for you. I'll come round now at once and cook it.'

'It's most awfully kind of you. I couldn't dream of troubling you. You've got plenty to do without cooking my lunch.'

'But I must cook your lunch. I can't let you starve. I'll pop it under the grill, it'll be done in two twos. I'm not busy just now – the children are out.'

'Oh, they're out, are they?'

At this, he immediately advanced, stepped over the threshold into her house, as if to say: 'Your dwelling-place is purged, safe for me.' But he glanced round, nose lifted, sensing the hated young in ambush still, ready to burst out with yell and gibe, a brandishing horde, and ride him down.

'Wait,' she said; 'we've got heaps of potato left over. I'll get it and fry it up for you, if you can spare a bit of lard.'

She went through the kitchen into the larder, seized the dish of cold mashed potato, winked at Mrs. Plumley, murmured: 'The hens can't have this, it's got to go to Captain Moffat. He's in trouble: Violet has let him down. I'm going next door to cook his chop. If you hear me blow a whistle, come at once.'

The kitchen door, closing again, cut her off from Mrs. Plumley's hilariously collapsing amplitudes.

'Here we are,' she said, bright. 'All ready.'

The telephone bell rang. She lifted the receiver and heard John's voice above a subdued bubbling and humming.

'Mummy? Look here, can you be along in five minutes?'

'No, I can't. Not possibly.'

'Why not? We're all set for the rehearsal.'

'Go on learning your parts for half an hour. I'll be along as soon as I can.'

'In half an hour?'

'Yes, with luck.'

He said disapprovingly: 'It holds us up rather. Make it as soon as you can, do. There's a hell of a lot to see to one way and another, and time's getting short.'

'You're telling me.'

'O.K. See you in half an hour *at latest*. Hold on, Gerald wants to speak to you.'

The bubbling ceased and the delirious voice of Gerald pounced upon her ear.

'That you, Mrs. Ritchie? I say, everything's going superbly; it really is. We've put up a wizard stage, and John and Oliver are doing the footlights to-night. And, I say, John's had some absolutely superb ideas for the noises off stage, and he's rigged up an electric bell, absolutely superb. He's worked like a black.'

'You think I can be proud of him?'

'*Rather*, absolutely… Mrs. Ritchie, could you possibly come along soon? – if you're not too frightfully busy? It's about our sketch. We frightfully want you to O.K. it before we begin rehearsing absolutely seriously. You see, the thing is, Oliver and I went to *Fast and Furious* in London last week – have you seen it? – it's absolutely *superb* – and to-day we had the idea of incorporating a bit of it in our sketch – you know, just roughly, not enough to have to ask the authors for permission, I shouldn't think The point is, do you think it's a good idea?'

'Well... I haven't seen *Fast and Furious* –'

'Oh, you really ought to –'

'But isn't it on the sophisticated side?'

'Sophisticated, yes,' he agreed, breathless. 'That's just it. It's incredibly sophisticated. Some of the jokes distinctly – you know –'

'Have you put in those particular jokes?'

'Well, as a matter of fact, we *have*. It's a thing about advertisements – three chaps – and the point is to put it over frightfully solemnly, with the chaps doing a bluff on the audience, you know, getting them all worked up into thinking something frightfully – you know – is coming, and then at the very end, when the audience is pretty well at breaking point, we simply roar out all together: '*Have you MacLeaned your teeth to-day?*' and the curtain comes down. At least, with luck it comes down.'

'I see.' Her head whirled. 'It sounds fairly innocent.'

'Oh, *grand*! You don't think we'll be hissed? – or even worse; that it might – sort of misfire? It went down like hot cakes in London, but of course a village isn't quite the same.'

'The village will relish any joke about false teeth. Or even B.O. they'd swallow without feeling too queasy.'

There was a second's pause.

'I see... Well... thanks most frightfully, Mrs. Ritchie. I dare say we could change it to that.' He sounded a little crestfallen, evasive.

She said quickly: 'Perhaps we're talking at cross-purposes. Wait till I come. I can't concentrate on the telephone. Listen, will you give your mother a message? Owing to unmentionable circumstances over which we have no control, there will be no film show. Will she please get on the track of that conjurer?'

'The conjurer. Yes, yes, rather, *superb*, I'll tell her at once. It'll be quite all right. Don't worry about anything, Mrs. Ritchie! Everything's going fine. Would you hold on a moment? Jane wants to speak to you.'

She waited. Nothing happened. The sound of breathing came through the receiver.

'Jane?'

'Mummy?' Constrained piping, dubious.

'Yes, I'm here.'

'Hallo.'

'Hallo, how are you?'

'Quite well, thank you,' said Jane, polite.

'What did you want to say to me?'

Bawling to overcome the mechanical obstruction between them Jane continued: 'Puffles is lost.'

'Who's lost?'

'Puffles. You know Meg's dog. He went off hunting and he hasn't come back.'

'I expect he will soon.'

'We don't think he will. Don't you know his eyes are bad? Meg thinks he's lost his way. Or else been picked up by some American soldiers.'

'Let's hope not. Would you be interested to know your trunk's come?'

'What?'

'Your trunk. I found it at Redbury.'

'Oh, good. *Don't unpack something done up in green paper in the corner at the bottom.*'

'All right.'

'Just leave it there. Don't touch it. Promise.'

'I promise.'

'Good-bye.'

'Good-bye – I'll be along soon.'

'If you can't find us, you'll know we've gone to look for Puffles.'

Injunctions, dissuasions rose to her lips. She suppressed them, and replaced the receiver. Captain Moffat was still standing in the same position, on the same piece of carpet, holding his plate. She thought irritably: 'Try a squib – why not?'– and said:

'It's very queer about young children: they telephone to you from half a mile away to ask if they can stay to tea, and their voices sound so sad and lost, they might be telling you they'll never never get home again. What happens?'

His withered face, immature and inexpressive as a youth's, contracted, wary: he worked the muscles of his jaw like a stammerer. In the rigid moment before his eyes left hers, she saw something wriggle, scurry in the two dark holes... Consternation of a wood-louse, crawling from a hole in the kindled log, scurrying to escape the hot threat.

Then he said, and his smile was quite friendly, quite engaging: 'Can't think how all you parents put up with it – all that gang of young toughs in and out all day. But I suppose you enjoy it. How d'you keep them fit on the rations, the rate they grow?'

'It's quite a job. But I do enjoy it.'

Carrying the dish of potato, she accompanied him down fifty yards of road to his Tudor cottage, with its tiny leaded panes, thatched roof, wealth of oak beams, sagging ceilings and other disheartening old-world features. He went before her into the kitchen, and said ruefully, acknowledging the forlorn debris of his breakfast – loaf, cup of tea, scrapings of the jam pot – still unwashed on the table:

'I'm afraid I'm awfully helpless.' With a faint shy smile he added: 'This is the first time my wife and I have been separated since the day we married.'

He turned his back on her in his embarrassment, opened the door of the frugal store-cupboard and looked in. She saw his straight athletic back and shoulders, the frail young-looking nape into which his brown hair tapered; and, between ear and temple, the twisted hollow of the wound through which, twenty-five years ago, the life spirit of Captain Moffat had been blown out of his head into limbo.

She said: 'I do love your wife.'

He turned round again and said emotionally: 'She's the kindest, best, most unselfish... No one knows what that girl does for others... And expects no thanks for it.'

'I know. She's so good. Her face is so good. I love it.'

The innocent plain face of Mrs. Moffat, lined, framed in grey hair, so ungirlish, hovered between them. Feeling, what with Captain Moffat's loneliness and the intimacies of domestic service to him, on the brink of deep waters, she nervously switched on the electric stove and went to hunt in the larder for a bit of fat.

'She's a saint,' he declared, when she came back.

She was his girl, he was her boy, her precious husband. It was having to counter, for so many years, the questions in his sunless head: 'What's the use of going on? Why not put an end to it all?'; the proof that must be given him over and over again that it was all worth while, they were together; it was the labour of driving foundations under him, of trenching him, roofing him, that had given Mrs. Moffat the drained look, the arrested smile of a face in an old photograph. But they enjoyed gardening, and taking long walks together, playing bridge, talking to their cats, listening to Tommy Handley and the Brains Trust; and Mrs. Moffat said serenely to her neighbours that nobody who had not suffered from nerves could understand them. Mrs. Moffat would see to it that she didn't die first.

'Tell her when she rings up,' she said, placing the chop on the grill, deciding to commit herself, 'she needn't worry about you.

Mrs. Plumley and I will see you're fed as long as she's away. If you don't feel like joining our noisy meals, we'll pop round with the rice pudding.'

Mrs. Plumley would undoubtedly feel her shoulders broad enough for this. Her opinion might be that the Captain ought to pull himself together and not put it all on his wife; but he was a man and helpless: her disapproval was mere lip service to the arid theory of women's rights. He didn't need to go down like he did, like we all could if we let ourselves; but when he was up you saw he'd been a nice-looking beggar with a bit of devil in him once. There'd be no harm in doing a bit of cooking for him.

'It's most awfully good of you,' he said, without any stiffness.

'I know she'd do the same for me,' she said, cheerful, over the potatoes, keeping the pitch down. 'That's one good thing that's come out of the war – at least for me. I mean, people like us really being neighbours. Knowing we can call on one another in a tight spot.'

Half an hour later she went along the lane that made a short cut through the fields to the Carmichaels'. The good turn done to Captain Moffat made her feel light-hearted. She had left him sitting down to a well-grilled chop and a crisp fry of potatoes, grateful, cheerful and perfectly equal, he said, to the washing-up. He had talked to her about sailing in a small craft to Norway when he was a boy. He would not come in to supper because he was expecting a call from Molly – yes, she had become Molly between one moment and the next – but he would look in about seven-thirty for a portion of macaroni cheese. She looked forward to the expression on the children's faces when she announced to them that she had been with Captain Moffat, cooking his lunch. The antipathy was mutual: they called him ghastly. But all that would be changed now: he would soon be saying: 'Jolly children you've got, Mrs. Ritchie (or even Margaret?). They would be saying he wasn't at all bad when you got to know him. He would offer to give them riding lessons... and one thing leading to another – new interests – old pleasures and activities resumed... Mrs. Moffat would confess to him her secret longing: to adopt a baby. 'By all means, dear; by all means. High time we had some young blood in the house.' Or better still, hey presto, Mrs. Moffat pregnant – why not? – only forty-two – one late last sprig, just not too late: Mrs. Moffat's woman's life fulfilled, the Captain's hope and pride given back to him. 'And all through you, dear.' All through friendship.

She checked her step sharply, and said aloud: 'Really, you're revolting.' Still this sickening self-indulgent daydreaming, this perpetual wash of emotional flotsam, blocking the channels of the clear flow of reason. No ideas, no intellectual progress, none. No wonder, perhaps, that Charles her husband had left her years ago, transferring his suitcases, his typewriter, his notes for a book on Marxist aesthetics and his affections to a clear-browed female research student in physics.

Spangled, studded with cold lucent buds, the hazel and elder bushes enclosed her path. Wild arum thrust in the banks; the ditches smelt of spring.

She opened Mrs. Carmichael's front door and saw Mrs. Carmichael in the hall, in the act of hanging up the receiver. She said: 'Margaret! Hallo, darling. I've just been talking to the conjurer.'

'You haven't!'

'Yes, truly. I've tracked him down, I've engaged him. He seemed awfully taken aback.'

'You sound rather doubtful about him.'

Mrs. Carmichael's eloquent brown eyes widened, dubious, wistful.

'He seemed so *drowsy*.'

'Perhaps he's just starting his summer sleep. I expect conjurers do the opposite of hibernating. I hope he won't muff his tricks.'

'He sounded – sort of old.'

'How old?'

'Very, *very* old.'

'It hadn't struck me, of course all the younger conjurers would be in the Forces?'

'It hadn't struck me either.'

'What a pity.'

'His name is *Feakes* – Mr. Cyril Feakes…'

'Have you definitely engaged him?'

'*Quite* definitely. Oh, yes…'

'Good for you. That's one load off our minds, anyway.'

'I think,' said Mrs. Carmichael, 'he was drunk.'

'Do you really?'

'Of course the line was bad… But he seemed to say something I didn't like the sound of.'

'What was it?'

'He said – I'm almost *sure* he said he'd start with twenty minutes' *vent*.' Her eyebrows went up, almost into her widow's peak. '*Can* he have said that?'

They stared at one another, aghast. Then suddenly: '*Oh!* Ventriloquism!' cried Mrs. Ritchie.

They collapsed in laughter, leaning against the wall.

'My *brain!*' wailed Mrs. Carmichael. 'It just doesn't *function* any more. Don't you think it's some vitamin deficiency – or the lack of fresh fish? John brought along our play this morning, and honestly I *have* tried, I took it up to my bedroom for an hour before lunch, but I simply *cannot* concentrate with all these animals going wrong, and the noise the children make.'

Struck by the silence of the house, Mrs. Ritchie listened, and said: 'Where are they?'

'The children? Oh, my dear…' Mrs. Carmichael put her little ringed hand to her forehead. 'They're all out, I think.' She looked vague, thoughtful, conscience-stricken. 'And we want to rehearse, don't we?'

'Where have they gone?'

'I'm afraid they've gone to look for Puffles. Meg got so worked up about him, and it seemed such a pity for them to stay indoors this lovely afternoon… To tell you the truth, I was so sick of the thumping on the piano, and that endless rolling about and knocking the furniture to pieces – what do they call it? – *mobbing* – I was only too thankful… Darling, you look tired: very nice, but tired. Let's sink down for a few minutes. They swore they'd be back by half-past three at the very latest.'

In the long, comfortable living-room with its sunny bay of glass and its attractive chintzes, they sank into armchairs, stretched their trousered legs out before them and closed their eyes.

'One cigarette,' sighed Mrs. Carmichael, 'then we might go through our parts? Perhaps if we *read* them together a few times it would seep into my head subconsciously? And to think I once recited "The Falls of Lodore" at school without a single mistake. Does your head always ache these days?'

'Always.'

'So does mine.'

'Does the conjurer know how to get here on Saturday?'

'I've told him to take that last bus out from Brading. But getting him *back* is another matter. If we could get him down to Redbury he could catch a train – if there is one. I wonder if Turnbull would come and fetch him. I suppose I'd better find out at once.'

She went away to telephone, and shortly returned saying: 'Mr. Turnbull says he'd oblige if he could but it's his fire-watching night, and if it turned out to be the – you know – *the* night, and he was to be absent from his post even for half an hour, you can imagine the results. How comforting it is when powerful things like garages and coal merchants don't refuse you with gloating glee, It sets one up almost as much as if they'd said yes.' With a return of her natural buoyancy, she examined her pretty face in a pocket mirror, re-decorated her mouth and said: 'Oh, well, if the worst comes to the worst, one of us will have to put him up. I wouldn't really mind, would you? He might be so interesting.'

'I'd mind terribly. And so would he. I'm sure it would be against the rules of the Magicians' Union. And don't you dare even hint such a possibility in front of the children, or we shall get no peace. Come on, we'd better run through our parts before they get back.'

They read through the sketch together three times, trying out varying shades of pitch, tempo and emphasis. Really, they agreed, there was no need to worry: the mere fact of seeing them on the stage would be rich comedy for the village, the crouching on hands and knees would cause a roar, and when it came to their both announcing their age as twenty-five, the house would come down. Mrs. Carmichael had the very thing, she remembered, in the way of an Edwardian straw hat of her mother's in a box in the attic; furthermore, she almost thought there was an old hip bath somewhere in the loft. With growing feelings of optimism and mutual affection they closed the book: the time was ripe for a proper rehearsal. They must practise the business, they would work at it till it came pat, and the words – the words would come of themselves. Should one break down, the other could prompt.

They retired to opposite corners of the room. Mrs. Carmichael advanced towards the fireplace for her first tricky piece of soliloquy. She started with dash, reversing the order of the sentences, hesitated, dashed on again, stumbled and was lost.

'Never mind; we'll go straight on. Begin at: "*Ah, my parcel!*"'

'*Ah, my parcel!*'

'Pretend you see it on the table.'

'*Ah, my parcel!*' Mrs. Carmichael's hands sprang forward, hovering in space a few inches above the table. She lifted nothing, put it down again, laid her hands flat on the table, bowed her head and shut her eyes.

'Never mind. It'll come. Now I knock at the door and come in.' She rapped sharply on the panelled wall and advanced. 'You say: "*Ah, the new lodger, I presume?*"'

'*Ah, the new lodger, I presume?*'

Mrs. Ritchie stopped. Mrs. Carmichael fixed her with a smile of maniac formality.

'All right, go straight on.'

They went straight on.

'*Ah! I see my parcel has arrived before me.* Now you say: "*Excuse me, that is my parcel.*"'

Giving her all to the expression, Mrs. Carmichael said it. They went on for half a minute.

'I've forgotten which my name is. Oh, yes. *I am Miss Arabella Browne.*'

'No, no, that's *my* name. You're Angelina. Let's go back to: "*Excuse me, you will see that it is addressed to Miss Browne.*"'

They went back; and almost at once dried up. Paralysed, they gazed at one another, their hands weakly clutching at nothing over the table.

A sound of whimpering at the garden door came to their ears; then a series of short sharp barks mounting to a piercing climax.

'Puffles!' Mrs. Carmichael flew to the door. Puffles, a stocky Cairn, came in, voluble, hysterical, mud-caked, straws in his hair. Rolling one eye on his mistress, he dragged his guilt along the floor.

'Oh, what a bad bad naughty boy! And a good good boy to come home before dark. Does he want his dindin?'

Mrs. Carmichael flew to fetch it for him. Wagging frenziedly, he devoured it, then, still wagging, took a hearty draught of water from his bowl, and retired to his basket to lick his paws.

'He gets his poor paws *so* sore,' said Mrs. Carmichael. 'That beastly Airdale he goes hunting with makes him do all the digging. What's the time? Half-past three already.' She looked thoughtful, went to the window and scanned the open landscape of wood-girt ploughland. 'I can't see a sign of them... You know, darling, I think I'd better go and look for them. They're probably going in circles in the wood, calling and listening down all the rabbit holes. You know what Meg is about Puffles. I *must* relieve her mind... Puffles stay in his beddy and have a nice long rest.'

They left Puffles composing himself for a nice long rest, went out through the garden, across the rough, flinty field – empty, as Mrs. Carmichael sorrowfully pointed out, of the form of Conker – and plunged into the beech-wood that flanked the Carmichael property.

'I'm much nearer to knowing my part than you think, darling,' said Mrs. Carmichael. 'I know I am. I'll be word perfect to-morrow and we'll have a whole day of concentrated rehearsing.'

Treading down beds of brown beech leaves, part crisp, part sodden, avoiding the fresh-sprung drifts of sorrel, wood-spurge, bluebell leaves, caught by wreaths of floating bramble, they reached the grassy, deep-rutted ride that ran, set with primroses, down the whole length of the wood. Flutingly Mrs. Carmichael sent her voice forth this way and that, calling her children's names. No reply. The blackbirds went on carolling and whistling in liquid riot high out of sight.

Talking of marriage, love, children, the war, they walked through insubstantial shafts, walls, columns of green light and violet shadow. They passed the place where, in 1940, a stray bomb, jettisoned, had fallen; where splintered tree-trunks, smashed branches, charred and jagged, still stuck up stark in a tumultuous crater of crushed chalk and lacerated roots: war's eye, sterile, violent and dead, staring even here, through fringes of milky shoots and the wildfire mesh in the locks of living branches.

Mrs. Carmichael called again; then Mrs. Ritchie called, then gave the family whistle. There was no answering coo-ee or whistle.

'They can't be here,' said Mrs. Carmichael. 'Bother, oh bother them.'

They came to the strange dyke, object of speculation to antiquarians, which ran through a section of the wood, slithered down it into a green cascade of bluebells, and clambered up on the farther side. Now they were standing on a higher terrace, where the tree-trunks were taller, closer, wider in girth. They stood still. The thick light had an odd quality, as if a white brilliance, like snow, were reflected in it from above.

'Look!' said Mrs. Carmichael.

They looked up and saw that, high above their heads, the crowns of six vast cherry trees in blossom intermingled with the roof of branches, pierced it, shot great luminous rockets through it into the sky. They could just see the tips of the boughs exploding in incandescent star-clusters against the blue.

'How could I have forgotten it was their time?' murmured Mrs. Carmichael, awestruck.

'Look!' Mrs. Ritchie put a warning hand on her arm.

They looked before them down a straight aisle, and saw, under the largest of the cherry trees, the back view of two brilliantly-clad figures, stretched out full length side by side on the ground. Their hands were clasped behind their heads, their feet were crossed, and each had a bunch of primroses and anemones on its stomach.

'Listen.' The sound of treble conversation, non-stop, reached their ears. 'No wonder they didn't hear us shouting.'

They advanced upon them without noise, and then softly called their names. Jane and Meg shot to their feet, scattering flowers.

'Hallo!' they said, startled, sheepish.

'What are you doing?'

'Nothing.'

'I suppose you forgot the time?'

'No,' they said on a note of query, as if mystified.

'We thought you'd like us to pick you some primroses,' said Meg.

'You know,' said Jane stiffly, 'you were wishing yesterday we would.'

They bent down and started to gather up their scattered bunches.

'We've been whistling and yelling for twenty minutes. I suppose you didn't hear us?'

'No!' they exclaimed, all honesty and amazement; and Jane added: 'I promise you we didn't.'

'Puffles has come back,' said Meg's mother.

'Oh, good! Jane, Puffles has come back. I thought he must have, as we hadn't found him.'

'Jane, what on earth have you got on?'

Jane was clad in a quilted scarlet jacket with a hood, a white sweater, and a flaring delphinium-blue skirt finished off with a broad red leather belt studded with silver. Everything was much too tight and much too short, but the effect was picturesque.

'It's Meg's skating costume she brought back from America. And Meg's got on her ski-ing costume, to make a pair.'

In truth, Meg was becomingly and totally encased in a trousered, zipped and belted garment of bright yellow woollen cloth, piped with crimson, with a hood to match.

'It was sweet of Meg to let you wear it, and you both look rather divine, but thank goodness your trunk's come, so perhaps you'd better fly back and change before you burst Meg's lovely skating suit beyond repair.'

'*Oh, not my old shorts and jumper!*' Jane's eyes dilated, expressing horror and anguish. '*I can't!* Roger's going to paint us both in these clothes to-morrow.'

'He likes them,' said Meg.

'They *are* rather attractive,' said Mrs. Carmichael, putting her head on one side and looking dreamy. 'By the way, where are they all? The boys?'

'Oh, Gerald and Oliver and John have gone home by the road. *Hours* ago. They were afraid they might be late for the rehearsal. I don't know *what* they'll do when they find you've simply gone out.'

'Roger's somewhere,' said Jane. 'He went to see if he could find some cherry low enough to pick.' A look of extravagant welcome spread suddenly over her face. 'Look, there he is, coming now.'

Roger Wickham, tall, slight, walking with the uncertain grace of his eighteen years, came through the trees towards them, carrying a huge sheaf of flowering cherry branches. He had a pale long cool-looking face, a fine head covered with wavy light-brown hair, beautiful secretive lips and clear eyes like aquamarines. They all looked at him smiling, and he smiled back, looking at none of them.

'I picked these for you,' he said, dividing his sheaf, giving half to Mrs. Carmichael, and half to Mrs. Ritchie.

3

'My *wedding* hat!'
'My *funeral* hat!'

On these words, a twofold wail of melodramatic woe, the rickety stage rocked and shuddered as John, in the wings, plunged upon the cords and propelled the curtains spasmodically together. Kneeling forward centre, still bearing aloft her share of a dripping Edwardian garden-party hat, she let her eyes slide through the dwindling space and observed, in the front row, seven dumbfounded adenoidal infants on their mothers' laps. Mrs. Groner of the Post Office, permitting her masterful features a faint relaxation; Old Arthur, impassive, dusky, primitive wooden idol in chiaroscuro, stuck with a pipe, sealing deafness thicker in a cloud of shag; Mrs. Fuller, washerwoman, mountainous, rocking, rolling, perspiring in unbridled appreciation of ladies' efforts: yes, all were there to watch her *début*. Blest pair of curtains, with a last convulsion their red plush folds flounced together and penned her safe from the many-headed monster. Clapping? Yes, loud, genuine clapping. Can it be that I am frightfully good at theatricals? She knelt back at ease on her knees, dropped the glutinous leghorn mass, and leaned across the zinc bath, arms outstretched, to embrace her fellow-actress. At this moment the stage rocked madly on its trestles, John crash-landed beside her, bellowed in her ear: '*Get up, for God's sake! Take a bow!*' and in one bound hurled himself into the wings and upon the cords again. This time the draperies whisked back as if by daemonic propulsion, the humming cavern crammed with moony fungoid growths yawned once more upon her. She stood in smiles and embarrassment, nodding and blushing, aware of her companion bending low in a succession of stately acknowledgements beside her. The zoological odours of the blacked-out and unventilated community assailed her in a palpable tide, Old Arthur predominant. 'Good for you, 'M!' shrieked Mrs. Fuller. Curtain again. Gerald, Oliver, Meg, John and Jane surged from the wings to congratulate her.

'Superb, Mrs. Ritchie, *superb!* Incredible!'

'There Mummy, you didn't get a single word wrong. I was listening.' Jane clasped her. 'There, you see, you *can* act. The only thing was, your hair was untidy.'

Faint wonder crossed her mind that Jane and Meg should be wearing their pyjamas and dressing-gowns before she remembered that they were dressed for their parts. Their faces, made up by the expert hand of Mrs. Carmichael, gleamed in unnatural flawlessness, precious, lustrous as tropical shells.

'Well done, Mum.' Satisfied with her, wasting no words, John thumped her on the back.

'I'm not the one to congratulate.'

She broke out of the throng to hug her companion, who was modestly busy collecting the properties and shaking the ostrich feathers out over the bath. Her arms enclosed not the light slenderness of Mrs. Carmichael, but the square athletically upholstered frame of Audrey, the bank manager's sixteen-year-old daughter from Redbury. Was it only yesterday? – it was – that the telephone had rung at 7:30 a.m. and the broken voice of Mrs. Carmichael had quavered in her ear, announcing a sleepless night, expectation of nervous breakdown and total inability to master her part. She would do anything, anything to help: appear behind the footlights she could not. She was taking a day in bed to fit herself for every menial back-stage task that might be heaped upon her.

At eight o'clock trampings and murmurings arose from John's ground-floor bedroom, and shortly after, her door was flung open and John, in his dressing-gown, stalked heavily towards her bed. He said:

'Mrs. Carmichael has thrown her hand in.'

'I know. She's telephoned. Who told you?'

'Gerald and Oliver. They came round.'

'Where are they now?'

'Just outside.' He called over his shoulder, sour: 'You may as well come in,' sank on the bed, lay back and closed his puffy eyes, Short of sleep after three nights of setting up the stage, he was not quite himself.

'Mrs. Ritchie, good-morning! Are we disturbing you?'

They came in and advanced to the foot of the bed, greeting her and apologising with a gentlemanly combination of diffidence and *savoir faire*.

'The foundations of our lives have cracked overnight,' said Oliver. 'Our mother has let us down. We are simply adrift in the storm.'

'We thought,' said Gerald, assuming an expression of do-or-die practical responsibility, 'we'd better come round at once and discuss the position. Do forgive us for not having shaved.'

'How often do you shave?' said John with a flicker of interest.

'There's no position to discuss,' she said from the pillow. 'There's no sketch. It's off. Or do you think perhaps I might manage both parts myself?'

'*Oh!* – like Ruth Draper,' cried Gerald. 'Have you seen her, Mrs. Ritchie? She's *incredible*. She simply peoples the stage. If only you – I'm sure you –'

He broke off, looking thoughtful. Some private mental image caused him to break into a yell of laughter, rapidly suppressed. 'No... no... I suppose it wouldn't do.'

'We're incredibly sorry about Mummy,' said Oliver, speaking now with serious manly regret. 'I'm afraid her morale collapsed, we ragged her too much. Daddy woke us with the ghastly news before he started for the station. He's rather fed up, I'm afraid. I'm sure we could brace her up if we had the chance, but he's absolutely forbidden us to try.'

'I'm not worrying,' she said; 'I shall rest now.'

'Good, good, Mrs. Ritchie! Honestly, don't worry. I promise you everything will be all right. If the worst comes to the worst,

I'll send a wire to Daly to come at once. You know he plays the accordion superbly. Oh, and I almost forgot to tell you: *Roger plays the violin superbly*. We found our grandfather's violin in the attic last night, actually not broken, and he tuned it in no time and played absolutely any tune we asked by ear. It was incredible – wasn't it, Oliver? Honestly, Mrs. Ritchie, though she is our mother, between ourselves, it's turned out for the best. It became clearer and clearer to us – didn't it, Oliver? – that Mummy's sphere of usefulness lies elsewhere.'

John sat up.

'Dividing the time equally between the two parts,' he said, 'I compute that your mother's part runs for seven and a quarter minutes. Say four minutes of dialogue… absolutely elementary dialogue… three and a quarter of business.' He shrugged his shoulders.

'Minutes can seem years,' said Oliver. 'Obviously they seemed so to our mother conning her lines.'

His face went out of drawing, and he squinted at a point just above John's head. Thus far, no farther, said his squint. I have covered our dishonour with mockery: you shall not expose and scourge it. Gerald looked anxious. She gave John a shove with her foot under the bedclothes, and he fell back again.

'Oh, Mrs. Ritchie,' said Gerald, 'I've never been into your bedroom before. What an absolutely charming room you've made it. I adore pink for a bedroom – everything's such marvellous taste. Would this be an Augustus John?'[12]

'No. It's by a friend of mine.'

'A *friend* of yours? How *superb!*'

'Leave me now, dear boys. I have to get up.'

'Oh, Mrs. Ritchie, couldn't we bring you breakfast in bed? I'm sure you ought to rest.'

'Not this morning, thank you very much.'

'Come on,' said John. He got up, stretched himself, looked

down at her with a brooding speculative eye. 'Look, Mummy. Supposing…'

He had an idea. It was pinning her down helpless on the mattress. She made a movement to put the sheet over her face and waited, but he only repeated: 'Come on,' and led them out. In a few moments, hilarious shouts, upbraidings, squeaks and giggles from the other side of the wall told her that they had invaded Jane's room and were rousing her from slumber. Shortly afterwards one of them stumbled, fell down at the turn of the stairs, cursed and groaned. Another brief interval elapsed before Jane rose against the doorway in floral pyjamas, tousled, flushed with joy and astonishment.

'Fancy them coming round so early! Did you expect them? They were very crool, they took all my bedclothes off me. Mummy, has something new happened?'

When she came down twenty minutes later they had gone. Mrs. Plumley said John had taken a bowlful of porridge from the saucepan and gone off with the others on his bike. He hadn't said nothing of where he was off to.

At eleven they were back with Audrey. She had a small suit-case strapped to the carrier of her bicycle, and entered with a quiet, ministering expression. She had come to get them out of a hole. Her mother, she said, had agreed to spare her for two nights. Committing lines to memory presented her with no difficulties, and she was an old hand at theatricals. She would retire now to her bedroom – could she help Mrs. Ritchie make up the bed? – be word-perfect by lunch and be ready to rehearse by two o'clock. It had been John's idea. He knew her already for a woman nobly planned. His partner last summer in the Brading Junior Tennis Tournament, with many a *Hard luck!* and *Well tried!* she had shepherded his shocking inadequacy into the semi-finals. His eyes ran over her with a cryptic look; he went off whistling to the hall to finish a job on the footlights.

Only yesterday; and now she stood upon the stage, their saviour, as Gerald, Oliver, Meg, Jane, John assured her with varying degrees of volubility and emphasis.

'I don't know how you did it, Audrey,' said Mrs. Ritchie.

'I did it because I was determined to,' said Audrey. She lifted her chin. Her cheeks sprang out, muscular, resolute.

Now the piano had been hoisted on to the stage, once more the curtain struggled back, and standing beside Jane in the wings, she beheld Oliver in evening trousers and dinner-jacket, wandering up and down behind the footlights, directing a stream of patter at the audience. Invisible to her, the piano gave out a chord.

'That's Roger,' whispered Jane. 'Isn't he a good player? Some of the notes won't sound.'

In a soupy croak Oliver sang: *You must – remember this – A kiss – is just a kiss...* The accompaniment started to improvise in a different key and tempo. The fingers touching the instrument knew what they were about, wringing muffled but accomplished harmonies out of the twanging keys. Oliver stopped. The music rose in a crescendo of flourishes and stopped. An argument developed.

'What are they supposed to be doing?'

'Really, Mummy! It's their comic turn. They're entertainers. Oliver's a crooner and Roger's coming in all wrong on purpose.'

Another chord reverberated. At this moment a red-nosed music-hall charwoman in bonnet, shawl and trailing black petticoats, and carrying a bucket, whirled past Jane and herself, scrabbled on to the sugar-box that served for step, and with a bawl of: *'Can I do you now, sir?'* burst upon the stage.

The laughter came with a crack and a roar. Two rows of children in front got up and cheered. Everybody knew where they were now.

'Who on earth is that?'

'Gerald. Really, Mummy, have your eyes gone wrong? Or your brains? You knew they had to change it all and put in a bit of sort of *Itma*[13] when you said their other turn wasn't funny enough.'

'I'd forgotten. So many things have happened.'

The day before yesterday, summoned to approve their rendering of a sketch of veiled but unmistakable impropriety, plucked and reassembled from fervid memories of *Fast and Furious*, she had been obliged, amid the astonished protests of Jane and Meg, to veto it.

The stage was given over to rowdiness and horse-play. Clanking her pail, bawling *A kiss is just a kiss*, the char scurried round and round on hands and knees, the crooner tripped over her repeatedly and fell prone, she lunged with her scrubbing brush between the pedalling legs of the accompanist. She sat on his lap, leered at him, tickled him with the poppy in her bonnet.

'Roger has to go on trying to be polite and dignified,' explained Jane. 'They're making it all up out of their heads as they go along – do you realise?'

Howl after howl tore the auditorium. Whistles, jeers, cheers and catcalls flew from the nether region where the local youth barred the main exit in a menacing phalanx. Mrs. Ritchie caught a glimpse of Audrey in the opposite wings, watching the exhibition with a smile of deprecating indulgence.

'My God, the stage will come down.' She moved closer to John, by the ropes. 'Hadn't this better stop soon?'

'Why? It's going down like hot cakes.'

She saw Mr. Carmichael rise urgently from his seat in the fifth row and press towards them. His sons were now advancing upon and retreating from one another in the abandonment of a kind of apache dance. At rapid intervals Gerald flung his skirts over his head, revealing red woollen bloomers, hirsute calves, green socks and sock suspenders. The howls increased in frenzy.

'Get that curtain down at once,' commanded Mr. Carmichael.

Startled, obedient, John attacked the ropes. Mr. Carmichael fell back against the wall and mopped his forehead.

'They don't mind making fools of themselves,' he said faintly.

'It's wonderful,' she said, 'to be so completely unselfconscious.'

'They don't inherit their temperament from my side of the family,' said Mr. Carmichael. He added: 'My wife has French blood.' He sighed.

'Mrs. Ritchie, Mrs. Ritchie, was it frightful? God, I've never felt so embarrassed in my life. I thought the curtain would never come down.' His bonnet askew over one eye, the grease-paint streaming off him, Gerald peered with wild gasps into her face.

'I thought you were terribly funny,' said Jane.

'Oh, Jane! *Thank you*, Jane! Oliver, Jane thinks we were terribly funny.'

'Our father did not think so,' Oliver said, brushing dust in a cloud off his sleeves, shoulders and trouser legs. 'He is ashamed, and rightly, of his sons.'

'Oh, Daddy, where have you sprung from? Have you come round behind to congratulate us?'

'Get out of my sight,' said Mr. Carmichael.

Jane stiffened and took a sharp breath.

'Sorry, Daddy. Oh, Daddy, you ruined my performance. In the middle of my best line I suddenly saw your dear face in front and I simply dried up.' At the recollection Gerald let out a yell of laughter.

'Never in my life,' said Mr. Carmichael, 'have I been so appalled, so humiliated.'

'You would rather have seen us dead at your feet,' said Oliver.

Mr. Carmichael passed a handkerchief over his lips. Carefully blank, his eyes sought those of Mrs. Ritchie.

'Sir,' said John anxiously, 'would you make the announcement? There ought to be community singing going on – and the collection. If we don't start something soon, they'll start breaking the place up.'

Mr. Carmichael stepped forward to face an audience reeling on the verge of anarchy. Alarmed, overheated and exhausted, the infants gave tongue. The mothers rocked them violently or charged for the exit. The toddlers and junior scholars stood on benches wrestling and aiming catapults. In the school-leaving age-groups cramming the back rows, vulgar behaviour between the sexes developed. Mr. Carmichael held up his hand, and in the benign authoritative tones proper to the C.O. of the local Home Guard made his announcement.

John sprang forward to hiss into his ear:

'Tell them Roger's going to lead the community singing on his – your – the violin.'

Concealing surprise, Mr. Carmichael broadcast this message. John suddenly vanished.

'Mummy,' Jane tugged at her arm and drew her down. 'Do you like Mr. Carmichael?'

'Very much.'

'I suppose he's all right.'

'Let's go out in front and hear Roger play.'

'Good heavens, what are you thinking of? I can't be seen like this. Besides, John's given me orders to stand by the ropes while he gets ready.'

Mrs. Ritchie went out in front in time to see Roger Wickham part the curtains and take his place in front of them, faintly smiling, carrying a violin and a bow. The sight of him surprised the children into silence. He stood looking amused, diffident and confident, mysterious and romantic; and sounds of tender ejaculation rose immediately among the matrons in the body of the hall. Pointing his bow at the children, he said:

'I'll play something for you first. What do you want me to play?'

'*Roll out the barrel*,' squeaked a little girl.

'O.K. Mind you all sing at the top of your lungs.'

They didn't trust him yet, nor yet the thing he was lifting and tucking under his chin and laying the stick across. But next moment he'd got it working brisk and clear, the right tune, too, and they started to sing, and sang at the tops of their lungs, while he nodded to them and smiled.

'Good for you. What would you like next?'

Volleys of demands came up at him. Unperturbed, he gave them *Kiss me good-night, Sargeant-Major*; *Little Brown Jug*; *Underneath the Spreading Chestnut Tree*. A girl at the back called for *Lily Marlene*; then *Rosalie*; then *Marezy Doates*; then *Wish me Luck*. Mr. Croft, retired constable, suggested *Coming round the Mountain*. He played every thing. He teased them, joked with them, apologised to, encouraged them, while the collecting-boxes went round and the coins clinked.

Suddenly an elderly female voice called:

'Why don't you give the old ones a chance?'

It was Mrs. Groner. A dark wave of colour raced over her face and neck and she looked down, glaring at her lap. She was a shy woman, and many disappointments and bereavements had all but sealed her lips. More genially, two or three of her contemporaries took up the cry. Some of the old-fashioned tunes.

'What would you like?' He coaxed Mrs. Groner.

Reluctant, defiant, she said after a silence:

'Can't you give us *Annie Laurie*?'

'I'll try. If I forget it you must help me out.'

He waited, concentrating, for a moment or two, then lifted his bow. The line of the air soared and sank, effortless, true, sweet and mournful. He could play, he could certainly most agreeably play tunes on the violin. At first they listened, but when he came to the end of the air, raised his eyebrows, smiled and began it again, they started to join in. Husky, unpractised, droning and wailing voices, they all sang *Annie Laurie*. The young ones sat dumb. Mrs. Groner wiped her eyes. Old Arthur leaned forward, cupping an ear.

'Bless 'im!' said Mrs. Fuller, weeping freely, to Mrs. Ritchie, who had slipped into a temporarily vacant seat beside her. 'Can't 'e bring it out beautiful? Oh, 'e's lovely. You can see 'e's a rascal, too, by 'is eyes.'

'He's a wonderful boy.'

He caught sight of her from the platform and gave her a smile. He looked a little excited now, and very happy.

'Do you think 'e'd give us *Barbara Allen*?' said Mrs. Fuller. 'It was my mother's favourite.'

She called: '*Barbara Allen!*' But he did not know it.

'I'm very very sorry,' he said.

'Never mind, sir,' called Mrs. Fuller, loving, for fear he should fret.

The new shepherd, a handsome giant of a man, far from his native Scotland, got up and asked with courteous dignity for *Loch Lomond*. Roger played it, but though a few tried they could not call the words to mind, and in the end the shepherd stood up and sang it solo. *Me and my true love will never meet again*, he sang out, uninhibited, in a deep, musical baritone, *By the bonny, bonny banks of Loch Lomond...* Mrs. Ritchie had dissolved in tears.

'Thank you very much,' said Roger. 'You ought to be on this platform, not me.'

Greeting this as a fresh sally of wit, the youth at the back relieved the awkwardness of emotional tension by bursting into laughter.

'No, no, I mean it,' said Roger earnestly.

He means it, he means it, repeated Mrs. Ritchie to herself, feeling thoroughly overwrought, turning round in her chair as if to reassure the shepherd. But the shepherd looked perfectly impervious to wounds or proffered balms. He had enjoyed singing and had now sat down again, easing his vast shoulders and stuffing his pipe with deliberation. Her eyes travelled on and lit on Mrs. Plumley, in toque and fur stole. Larger than life-size to her blurred vision, split from ear to ear, Mrs. Plumley's face shone upwards upon Roger in a trance of ecstatic intimacy. Her denture appeared to have broken loose and to be gleaming by itself about an inch in front of its moorings.

From behind the curtains came a threefold buzz. Familiar with the sound through a week of experimental testing, she recognised it for John's portable electric bell.

'That's my warning,' said Roger. 'Lucky for me. I only know one more tune, and that's *The Londonderry Air*. Shall I play it?'

The desperate faces of Jane and Meg bobbed round the piece of material screening the wings, and she slipped from her place and sped towards them.

'I couldn't think where you were,' said Jane. 'I hope to goodness nobody saw me peeping.'

'Mummy's gone home to get the party ready,' said Meg.

'And Daddy's counting the collection. I've got a feeling I've forgotten my part.'

'I'm shivering with nerves,' said Jane. Her hand was clammy.

'Everything's all right. You both know your parts perfectly and you look sweet. Remember to speak up.'

'Hark at them clapping Roger,' said Jane. 'They won't clap us like that.'

Roger stepped down on to the sugar-box, smiled at them, said: 'Good luck,' and went to take up his position as deputy curtain-puller. Jane's face relaxed for a moment as he passed, then froze again.

'Mummy, remember where I told you to stand. When I have to jump back to the side when the lights go out and the face comes at the window. I shall put out my hand behind me to see if you're there, and *mind you take it.*'

'All ready!' John leaped from the stage, balancing his calm on a knife-edge. He thrust the typed-out prompt copy into her hands, said to the little girls: 'Get on up and take your places'; to Roger: 'When I shine my torch three times, pull'; and vanished.

The curtain went up on the last item – *The Haunted House*, a Mystery, written and produced by Gerald and Oliver Carmichael and John Ritchie. Played by Meg Carmichael, Jane Ritchie, Gerald and Oliver Carmichael. Crashes, knockings, groans, moans, strange lights, ghostly apparitions and other mysterious effects by John Ritchie.

4

It took some time to remove the green substance, a paste of his own invention, from John's face. Lit by an arrangement of electric bulb, flex, and battery hung about his person, it had given blood-curdling effect to his recent impersonation of a corpse behind the curtain. After the application of an entire pot of vaseline, it still adhered to his cheeks in scabrous patches. Brushing his mother's hovering hand away, he tore them off at last, skin and all, presented a distressingly raw and inflamed appearance, and gave off a powerful smell of plasticene and gum fixative.

'Hurry, hurry!' said Jane. 'We're missing some of the party. Everybody else has gone on.'

'Do you want me to take off your make-up?' said Mrs. Ritchie.

'No, leave her alone,' said John. 'She looks quite decent for once.'

Jane's flawless mannequin mask incongruously surmounted the high plain neck-line, the ungarnished bodice and box-pleated skirt of her best pink silk uniform frock. At this brother's tribute, the eyes in the mask dilated in a wild flash and roll of gratification.

Plunging into his jacket, John added: 'Why can't she always make up?'

'Ten seems a bit young.'

'Meg says girls not much older than her do in America,' said Jane. '*Even at school*. Miss Potts would simply die if she heard such a thing.'

'Come on,' said John. 'God, I'm hungry. Leave everything. Gerald and me are going to clear up to-morrow. May as well take this, though...'

He buzzed his portable electric bell a couple of times, pocketed it, lingered a moment by the switchboard to touch it with loving fingers, and followed his womenfolk into the auditorium. Not an urchin remained in the hall, not one member of the local Dogs' Group prowled stiff-stepping in neurotic umbrage round the entrance. Not one footstep in the lane. The entire community so lately bursting the pitch-pine ark had vanished and, leaving behind a shroud of complex exhalations, become embedded in the soundless night. Features of heroes, calls to patriotic spending blazed and trumpeted at no one from the posters. The multi-coloured paper banner executed by the school children and tacked to the middle beam cried *Salute the Soldier!* into empty space.

They switched off the last lights, locked the door behind them, and were out in the dark.

'Walk on slowly,' said John. 'I must just collect my bike.'

Hand in hand, Jane and her mother sauntered down the lane in the direction of the Carmichaels' house. On either side of them, the hawthorn hedges condensed the thick of night in their long slumbering palisades.

'I should almost like to go for a long walk in the dark with you,' said Jane. 'Yet I want to get to the party. I know what there's going to be: *ice-cream*. Yet I keep thinking once the party starts we're getting nearer to the end of it. Then what shall we have to look forward to?'

'There's the sports next week.'

'Ah, yes, I forgot. But I'm afraid Roger won't be able to stay for them. He's going to start painting me and Meg properly at eleven o'clock to-morrow. Do you think I'd better keep my make-up on?'

'I think not, on the whole. Painters often prefer ordinary skin colour for girls.'

'But he may not be that kind. He may think – you know – you heard what John said... Will you ask him?'

'I'll ask him... What can that boy be doing? Is he making a bicycle? We'd better wait here for him.'

Emerging from the lane at the cross-roads, they halted by the edge of the triangle of rough grass called Four Points Green. Here the country expanded wide and full. After all, it was not dark. They could see the ghost roads raying out into far spaces of downland and valley, the shapes of horses in a nearby field, the five elms at the field's edge posturing dramatically like giants distraught. Overhead an amorphous patch of clouded incandescence showed the place of the obscured moon. An even lucent greyness suffused the air.

'The moon looks like a junket,' said Jane, staring upwards, 'when we've all had some, and there's only shreds and watery stuff in the bowl.' She sighed. 'I suppose Mr. Carmichael isn't bad really?'

'What's on your mind about him?'

'Well, he doesn't seem very kind to Gerald and Oliver. Ordering the curtain down on them. After all, they were doing their best.'

'But he wasn't angry with them. They weren't a bit upset.'

'Was it joking?'

'Yes. He just thought they were getting a bit rough.'

'I see. But he might have said: "Well done, boys, you made everybody laugh," or something like that. Still, Meg says he's all right when you get to understand his ways.' She put an arm round Mrs. Ritchie's waist. 'I'm glad I don't have to understand your ways.'

A series of muffled buzzes warned them of John's approach.

'Where's your bicycle?' said Mrs. Ritchie.

'Stolen.'

'*Stolen!* Where did you leave it?'

'Round by the back of the hut, I suppose, or in front. I don't know. I've hunted everywhere.'

'Round by the... where anybody could... How could you be so careless?'

'Heaven knows I had enough to think of,' he said, bitter, 'without remembering to padlock my bike to my person. Well, come on. There's nothing to be done about it. I can always borrow yours. May the thief find my saddle even more filthily uncomfortable than I did.'

He started to walk on, his shoulders hunched. Respectively worsted in a telephone engagement with Redbury Chief Constable, printing a neat notice in coloured chalks (four different colours for L O S T) to put in Mr. MacBean's window, in silence his mother and his sister followed him.

Suddenly Jane said:

'You never had it!'

'Never had what?'

'Your bike. Don't you remember? – you had to walk because of the suitcase with the properties in. You left it at the Carmichaels'.'

'So I did. Why on earth couldn't you say so before? All this flap for nothing.' He let out an eldritch whoop, and in a spirit of encouragement caught his mother a whack across the shoulders. 'Poor old Ma. Saved again. Cheer up.'

They struck into Mr. Carmichael's top pasture and started across the blanched insubstantial expanse towards the house.

'Well, it's over. We've won through,' said Mrs. Ritchie. 'Really, I do congratulate you. Your sketch went with a bang. Acting honours definitely go to you.'

'Mrs. Fuller enjoyed it, I'm pretty sure,' said Jane.

'I think everybody did,' said Mrs. Ritchie.

'Mrs. Fuller showed it most. She kept calling out. Mrs. Groner didn't show it at all. Nor did old Arthur – but I don't suppose he heard. Did Mrs. Plumley show it?'

'Oh, yes. She never stopped laughing.'

'Even in the frightening parts?'

'There weren't any,' said John. 'It was one stupendous side-splitting farce from beginning to end.'

'She laughed in Roger's violin-playing,' said John. 'Some of it wasn't meant to be funny. I hope he didn't see her.'

'She laughed out of love for him,' said Mrs. Ritchie. 'You know how she does.'

'Ah, yes. Like she laughs at the hens.'

'Or you,' said John.

'Is that it?' said Jane. 'I've often wondered why she laughs when I go into the kitchen. Mummy, did the clapping sound loud after our sketch?'

'Very loud.'

'I didn't seem to hear any. *You* got a lot of clapping, Mummy. I think you got most. At least – after Roger.'

'You put up a jolly good effort,' said John. 'But Audrey was ghastly. She simply missed the whole point.'

'That wasn't her fault. The only point was the spectacle of me and Mrs. Carmichael teamed up as a couple of young ladies. Who thought of Audrey? Who rushed off without a word to fetch her?'

'And she didn't forget any of her part,' said Jane. 'At least she only got a few words wrong.'

'She can't act for toffee,' said John.

'She thinks she can,' said Jane, surprised at this verdict.

'She would,' said John. 'I shouldn't be surprised to hear she's got her Girl Guides' badge for Dramatic Proficiency.'

'Do you think she has?' said Jane.

'She did rather seem to feel she was being a good influence,' said Mrs. Ritchie. 'If I'd dried up, I think I could have counted on her to say Bad luck! – audibly.'

John uttered a brief hoot of laughter.

'John loathes her,' said Jane. 'Don't you, John? He calls her Fatima. Behind her back, of course. I think she's very kind. It's kind to say Bad luck. And she mended my white party socks. She told me she's used to children, because she's got a little brother.'

'Oh, well, she came in useful,' said John. 'We'll give her three rousing British cheers to-morrow when she pedals away.'

'If she pedals away. I have an impression she feels there is much still to be done among us. I warn you: I will not endure any more helpfulness from anyone.'

'I'll deal with her,' said John. He gave his sister a nudge and said imploringly: 'Don't say it, don't. Keep it back. Just this once.'

'How do you know what I was going to say?... Anyway, I did think it was' – she added in a mutter – 'right to be helpful.'

John threw back his head with a light howl.

'So it is,' said Mrs. Ritchie. 'Don't tease her, John.'

'She's rather greedy, I must say,' said Jane, plumping at the last moment for the nasty spirit of the thing. 'Did you notice the helps of honey she took at tea?'

'The conjurer!' said Mrs. Ritchie quickly, 'I clean forgot about the conjurer. I was too busy to watch him. What was he like?'

'He was absolute hell,' said John. 'About ninety-eight, and a line of patter out of the Ark.'

'He was rather rude,' said Jane, prim.

'Rude?'

'Well, he got Cissie Hoddinott up on the platform and tried to make her shake hands with his – with Jack.'

'Jack?'

'His beastly doll,' said John.

'She didn't want to much,' continued Jane. 'But she did. And he kept saying: "Come along now, a nice squeeze, don't be shy. Call that a squeeze? Give him a nice squeeze like you give your boy-friend." As if she had one! She's only seven.'

'Oh, dear, how dreadful!'

'And at the end he said the – Jack was going to sing *The Bluebells of Scotland*, but he didn't, he sang a bit of *Tipperary*. I can't think how it happened.'

'He was blind drunk,' said John.

'No!'

'Well, squiffy. He kept on knocking over the glasses of water he was doing his drivelling tricks with.'

'Oh, his tricks were super,' said Jane. 'I couldn't see how he did any of them.'

'They were putrid,' said John. 'I could have done better myself with a week's practice. However, the kids enjoyed them. There was one ghastly youth who would keep going up on the platform and showing off – I can't think who he was – crowing out that one glass had a false bottom and he'd seen Feakes slip the handkerchief up his sleeve. Thinking himself jolly smart. Feakes obviously wanted to murder him. I don't blame him.'

'Well, I hope he got away all right in time for the last train,' sighed Mrs. Ritchie. 'Mrs. Carmichael swore she'd see to it.'

'Not a hope, I shouldn't think,' said John. 'There was some sort of muddle with the taxi.'

'Then he's walking back to Brading. Twelve and a half miles.'

'It's no good worrying,' said John. 'Perhaps he got a lift.'

They were through the gate, out of the field, and walking up the Carmichaels' drive. As they reached the front door, a figure standing before it moved aside and mumbled:

'Good-evening.'

'Oh, Captain Moffat! I nearly walked into you.'

'I've rung several times,' he said. 'Can't seem to make anybody hear.'

'I think we're expected just to open the door and walk in. Probably there's too much noise going on for anyone to hear the bell,' said Mrs. Ritchie, cheerful, laying a hand on the latch. A prolonged rumble as of feet galloping up and down uncarpeted stairs, shouts, shrieks, yells of laughter came to their ears.

'No, no,' said Captain Moffat urgently, almost laying a detaining hand upon her arm. 'I won't come in. I can't possibly stay. Mrs. Carmichael very kindly asked me to join the party, but I can't possibly. I only came along to pay my respects. Perhaps you would explain to her: I've had a rotten headache all day. I think I'll cut along home. Besides, I'm expecting a telephone call. You might tell her that, would you? I'm expecting a call.'

'From your wife?'

'Yes, yes.'

'Oh, we're missing it, we're missing it,' broke in Jane, in a frantic whisper. 'I'm sure they've started to play Murder.'

Captain Moffat muttered on through closed teeth: 'I wrote to her yesterday and told her she'd better come back. I don't like the idea of her being up in town. Those last raids were child's play to what's coming, so I hear. They might start any moment. I can't have her exposing herself to them. Besides' – his voice went up into his nose, weak with self-pity – 'I can't see to everything myself day in day out like this. There's all the potatoes to go in. It means too much stooping for me.'

'Can she leave her aunt?'

'She'll have to make some arrangement. That's what it comes to. I told her so in my letter. Dragging on like this. When all's said and done, I told her, she's got to consider her own health. It would be a nice how d'ye do if she broke down. These last two days, I don't know why it is, I've been completely deaf in one ear. Stone deaf...' His voice trailed away.

In pregnant silence John began to apply his weight to his mother's shoulder, edging her towards the door.

'I'm so sorry, Captain Moffat. I'm sure your wife will take the first train home to-morrow and all your troubles will be over. If only her poor aunt – it would be best if the end were to come for her poor aunt as soon as possible, wouldn't it?'

'It would be a happy release,' he said, brightening for a moment. 'It's all been very trying for us.'

'It's trying all round really, isn't it? Good-night, Captain Moffat. I'll tell Mrs. Carmichael. She'll be so sorry, but she'll understand. I hope you enjoyed the show a little bit?'

'Tell you the truth,' he said, 'I didn't turn up.'

'Oh, and you promised.'

He made a sound of nervous laughter.

'It looked so uncommonly like rain, I thought I'd better not risk turning out. Besides, I'm not much good in a crowd. An over-heated atmosphere tries me very much.'

He stood, he stood, he blocked the drive, the door; he was a dead man behind them hanging from the strangled moon, slumped against the door in front of them, against the way to light and sound. He fixed her in the dark with his sightless eyes; the enormous force of his negative energy held her rooted. John turned the handle, pushed her in with Jane and shut the door rapidly upon him.

They stood in total darkness. From the stairs and the landing came creakings, a muffled giggle. All round them invisible bodies breathed loudly, hemmed them in.

'It's Murder,' whispered Jane, despairing. 'It's started. I knew it.'

From six inches away arose a subdued enthusiastic bubbling.

'Mrs. Ritchie? Hallo! Jane? John? Good, good, superb. Gerald here. We've just started the second murder, you're just in time. Here, Jane, hold my hand, I need moral support. Mrs. Ritchie, would you care to join in? Daddy's playing, he's somewhere. If not, Mummy's in the drawing-room. She refused to play. I'm so sorry we can't turn the lights on, but perhaps you could manage to grope your way?' He bawled: 'Pax for a few moments! No murder till Mrs. Ritchie's passed.'

Mrs. Ritchie stepped cautiously down the passage. Somebody rushed past her and tumbled up the stairs. From above, Meg squeaked. A hidden agency opened the drawing-room door in front of her. The voice of Mr. Carmichael murmured a deprecatory greeting. She whispered, arch:

'Are you the murderer?'

'*Aaa-ha! Wouldn't you like to know?*'

He sounded quite… really so very… quite unlike himself; such a tease, so curiously uninhibited, so close in the dark. Where were his hands? The skin crawled on her neck. She nipped past him in a hurry and shut the door.

'Claire?'

But for the smothered glow of a log fire, here too all was lapped in shade.

'Margaret! I'm over here on the sofa. Do forgive me. I'm forbidden to show a light, though I'm sure there's nobody secreted in this room. Can you possibly find your way?' Mrs. Ritchie found her way and sank upon the sofa beside her. 'That's right, darling. Lie the other end and put your feet up like me. You must be worn out. I am. I feel I must sink while they play this dreadful game. Actually I don't suppose they'll ever stop. I've known them go on for two hours and a half, and sometimes I can't help wondering if it's good for them. They seem to get such a strange flush and glitter. Still, it makes entertaining beautifully easy.' She yawned.

Next moment, a prolonged blood-curdling screech appalled their ears. Somebody sprang up smartly from the window seat and galloped to the switches. Light flooded the room, revealing Audrey in the act of flinging open the door. 'Stay where you are, everybody!' she called; and marched forth into the now illuminated beyond to view the crime. The form of Oliver was seen to be stretched prone in the hall. The others stood against the passage wall or peered over the banisters. An indescribable babble was going on.

'*Boo!!!*'

Mrs. Ritchie and Mrs. Carmichael leapt violently. The sofa was convulsed throughout its frame as the figure of a small boy shot up from behind it and, with this disagreeable exclamation, rendered full blast, revealed himself.

'Oh, Norman,' said Mrs. Carmichael, icy, 'what a fright you gave me.'

'Aha! I thought I'd give you a start. You didn't know I was there, did you? I've been there all the time.'

He came and capered before them on short stout legs; twisting himself double, cackling with triumph.

'If there's one thing I *cannot* bear,' said Mrs. Carmichael, 'it's someone bouncing out on me and saying "Boo!"'

He cackled the more. His knees, between hairy grey stockings and grey flannel shorts, protruded aggressively. Mrs. Ritchie saw him in her mind's eye bundled into a belted navy blue raincoat, topped with a striped school cap, beating out tunes with his boots, loudly whistling, hanging out of the window of a crowded railway carriage. He tore from the room to join the others, shouting: 'I gave them such a fright! I was behind the sofa all the time and they never knew!'

'Nobody will take the slightest notice of him,' remarked Mrs. Carmichael.

'Who on earth?'

'My dear, it's Audrey's brother. It struck me at the very last minute I *must* ring up her parents and invite them, but luckily they had colds and didn't feel like it. But Mrs. Parker said Norman was so very keen to come, only she didn't like him bicycling back alone in the dark. So what could I do but offer to put him up? After what Audrey's done for me. He turned up at tea time, and everyone has completely ignored him. I've scolded Meg, but it's no use. She says he needs squashing. It does seem bad manners.'

'He doesn't seem to feel the squashing.'

'He's not very attractive,' sighed Mrs. Carmichael. 'But boys of nine or so are always repulsive, don't you think? He enjoyed the show anyway.'

'Oh!' Light dawned. 'He's the boy John was so withering about who went up on the stage and saw through all the conjurer's tricks.'

'Oh, dear, yes. I'm afraid poor Mr. Feakes got rather upset.'

They fell silent.

'Do you think he caught his train?' said Mrs. Ritchie gently.

'He *cannot* have,' said Mrs. Carmichael. 'The taxi didn't turn up till twenty past – it had another job – and the train goes at ten past. It doesn't bear thinking of.'

'Perhaps the taxi took him to Brading.'

'No. The man particularly said it was out of the question. He hadn't the petrol. He came from East Marling, you know – as a special favour. However,' she added, looking on the bright side, 'I gave Mr. Feakes a cheque on the spot, so that's off our minds.'

They came bursting through the door, all talking at once. Mr. Carmichael followed them, with an expression of mild satisfaction.

'Mummy, Mummy, your husband, our father, slew his first-born.'

'Ugh-gh-gh! I nearly died,' said Meg, falling into an arm-chair. 'I felt somebody's hot breath on my neck.'

'It was only me,' said Jane, falling beside her. 'I was trying to find you for company.'

'Jane's breath is always scorching,' said John. 'Like wild animals. Reeking of carrion.' He sauntered over to the refectory table at the end of the room and looked with absorption at the plates of buns, sandwiches and cakes, the bowls of trifle and preserves.

'I was the only one who stayed in here,' said Norman in his singularly strident treble. 'I saw you all sneaking out so I jolly well stayed behind. Look, I was just here, behind the sofa. Look!'

The two girls wreathed in the arm-chair glanced stonily in his direction, looking away again, toying with each other's lockets, their enamelled profiles laid side by side. Mr. Carmichael mixed three rum cocktails, and presented the ladies with one apiece. Roger met his own reflection in the mirror above the mantel-piece, smoothed his plumey hair.

'Who's for one more murder before we eat?' cried Gerald. His mother's protest was drowned in a chorus of acclamation, and he started to deal the cards round. 'Mrs. Ritchie, you must play this time.'

'No, no, I really won't. Not for a thousand pounds I wouldn't.'

'Oh, Mummy, you must,' began Jane. She pulled a card from the pack, glanced at it, laid it gently down in her lap and sat silent, placid, with transparent extroverted eyes.

Mr. Carmichael had the detective's card. Once more the lights were extinguished; with creak and padding tread the company dispersed. The parents relaxed and talked in low voices, sipping their drinks.

'How much did we make?' said Mrs. Ritchie.

'Sixteen pounds eleven shillings and sixpence,' said Mr. Carmichael. 'Really a remarkable effort for a small village. There wasn't a child who didn't put in sixpence at least; and there were a surprising number of notes. Remarkable.'

Mrs. Ritchie repressed the wish to say that she had put in a pound. What had the Carmichaels put in? No doubt Jane would have inquired of Meg and obtained satisfaction.

'How splendid,' said Mrs. Carmichael. 'What a grand start off to the week. It shows how much they enjoyed it. It *was* a success, thank goodness. We did deserve a success, didn't we? We've all worked so hard. I do hope there won't be jealousy.'

'Nerves are getting frayed on the committee,' said Mrs. Ritchie. 'I hoped we could avoid class antagonism by having half gentry, half village, but it seems to be working out the opposite way. What it comes to is, the village feel we ought to be running it all for them. They're alarmed, I suppose, at the responsibility. If we butt in they think we're patronising and if we retire they think we're snobbish. Both ways they're resentful.'

'My dear, I *know*,' said Mrs. Carmichael. 'Poor Mrs. Jessop – you know she's helping Mrs. Minchin run the Social – her husband rang me up in an awful state after lunch. She'd retired to bed in tears, he says he'll never let her lift a finger for the village again. She spent all morning making rock cakes and popped down herself with them to Mrs. Minchin before lunch. What do you think? Mrs. Minchin opened the door, took the whole tray and threw them at her head.'

'*No!* Why?'

'Oh, a lot of stuff about having left all the dirty work to her Dorrie, and who was going to see that the band got drinks, and of course we'd all be too stuck-up to come to the Social – and I don't know what. She's a bit mad, of course.'

'It's the change, Mrs. Plumley says,' murmured Mrs. Ritchie.

'Now I suppose we'll *have* to go,' sighed Mrs. Carmichael. 'And if we do they'll feel awkward and be on their best behaviour. What a pity it all is... Oh, and Mr. Parkinson resigned from being Treasurer. He says Mrs. Hoddinott accused him of embezzling her raffle money. He says Mr. Jebb can damned well take it on. But who's going to tackle Mr. Jebb? Margaret, would you? You might sort of joke him into it. You always make things sound so amusing.'

'Tell him you want to lay a problem before him for spiritual guidance,' said Mr. Carmichael.

At this moment they heard a distant stir, a shift behind the sofa.

'*Mon Dieu!*' said Mrs. Ritchie after a short pause, '*vous n'allez pas me dire, par exemple, que ce maudit garçon est encore là?*'

'*En effet,*' said Mrs. Ritchie. '*Tout prêt à sauter sur nous.*'

'*Tuons-le immediatement,*' said Mrs. Carmichael.

'*C'est qu'il a peur, sans doute.*'

'*Vous croyez?*' said Mrs. Carmichael; adding in a half-hearted way: '*Pauvre petit.*'[14] Then she said clearly: 'Hallo, Norman. Are you there again? Do you want to come and sit beside us?'

Silence.

A howl rose from the hall. Mr. Carmichael switched on the lights and went to do his duty. Unassumingly this time, Norman emerged from behind the sofa.

'Well, I may as well come out,' he said. He slid a glance at his hostess, and added with careful flatness: 'You gave me away to the detective, so there's not much point in my joining them for the investigation.'

'Norman, how awful of me. I didn't think.'

'It's all right.'

He bore no malice. He had his sister's ruddy springing cheeks and rubber mouth. With these, with his light-brown glass eyes, chubby jutting nose and chin, and general appearance of being coated with a layer of varnished know-all jauntiness, he looked not unlike Mr. Feakes' Jack. Yet many, thought Mrs. Carmichael, noting this, would call him a jolly little beggar, keen, the right stuff.

'Still, I might as well,' he said; and took himself off, leaving the two ladies to exchange conscience-stricken grimaces.

'We have humiliated him,' said Mrs. Ritchie. 'Never mind. It's something to know he has human sensibilities.' Back swirled the horde around them. Roger came and perched gracefully on the arm of the sofa beside Mrs. Ritchie.

'I do congratulate you, Mrs. Ritchie. Jane's grip on life is remarkable, you need have no fears for her future. I shall bear the marks for many a long day,' he added as Jane, flushed, exultant, came to join them.

'Jane, you don't mean to say you murdered Roger?'

'I was determined!' cried Jane, fixing him with starry eyes. 'I waited ages beside you at the bottom of the stairs, to put you off. I knew it was you because I felt your corduroy trousers; you're the only one wearing them. Then I went up on the landing and waited there another long time, then I crept down again quiet as a mouse, but *you'd* moved by then and I had an awful time finding you again. I nearly got somebody else. I think it was John –'

'I'll say it was,' said John. 'I felt her horrible clammy paws paddling on my face. I nearly let out a yell.'

'And at last I got you!' continued Jane. 'I wasn't sure if I'd be able to reach your neck, but I did.'

'You did,' said Roger. 'Undoubtedly you did.' Ruefully he stroked his windpipe. 'I've had some bad nightmares in my time, but nothing to equal that grisly moment.'

'A promising criminal, your daughter,' said Mr. Carmichael, grave, stroking his moustache. 'I rather fancy myself as an amateur sleuth, but she completely took me in. That look of perfect innocence when I questioned her – not overdone, mind you, just simple childish honesty – coupled with a capacity for lying which I can only describe as –'

'Barefaced,' said Oliver, whirling upon them with plates of buns and sandwiches. 'Our father can only describe it as barefaced. Jane, Jane, you've shaken our father's faith in girl-hood. His imagination boggles.'

Jane collapsed upon the sofa and buried her gratification and her bun in cushions.

Rapidly the generous board was stripped, draughts of cider and ginger beer were tossed down. Cider, surely, was heady stuff? She saw John in conversation with Roger lean back against the mantelpiece and make as if to prop his head upon his hand. His elbow slipped, he replaced it carefully, looking puzzled. One eyelid drooped, he was repulsively pale. Side by side at the buffet, the back views of Audrey and her brother displayed a striking family resemblance: square-planted, com-placent, humourless. Methodically they ranged over the table, clearing it of its remains. The little girls sat together, their bare legs crossed, on a small couch at the end of the room, licking ice-cream off little spoons daintily, like cats, and conversing in serious undertones. Mr. Carmichael put on his spectacles, took up a gardening catalogue and composed himself in his armchair. Oliver thumped upon the piano; his mother lay back, her eyes shut, tapping out the tune with one foot. The party was petering out.

'Jane,' said Mrs. Ritchie, 'when you've finished your ice –'

'What when I've finished my ice?' Jane shot upright.

'Time to go home.'

At this announcement, amid yells of protest, the party sprang to life and began to ascend once more in giddy spirals. Gerald dashed back into the room after a prolonged absence.

'Sorry, everybody, I was telephoning. Mummy, I got Daly long distance in ten minutes, wasn't it superb? He may be coming on Monday for a night or two, with a friend. Is that O.K.? Oliver, stop that filthy row. Let's have some decent music.'

He switched on the wireless. A husky voluptuous moaning, a swooning and a throbbing began to seep discreetly from the instrument. 'Reynaldo and his Dreamy Boys! Superb!' he cried.

'Why don't you dance? Do dance,' said Mrs. Carmichael faintly.

'Come on then.'

Gerald swung her to her feet and began to revolve. What he lacked in skill he made up for in enthusiasm, and soon she began to smile, to sparkle and look young again. Presently everybody was dancing. Rocking in a stately restrained way in the arms of Mr. Carmichael, Mrs. Ritchie beheld Oliver, John, Meg and Jane locked together in a close ring, arms intertwined, stamping and shuffling: a crude performance. Norman was not among them. He sat on a chair against the wall, munching the last rock cake and looking sleepy. Threading hither and thither, deft, smooth-turning, Roger guided Audrey. He looked as if he knew all about how to dance; and Audrey, bouncing light as a balloon against him – yes, Audrey could dance too.

Nostalgic and deprecating, Mr. and Mrs. Carmichael now took the floor together. Gerald and Oliver danced with the little girls. 'That's right, Jane, *superb*, you're getting it,' cried Gerald, while Jane, stiff, demure, eyes on the ground, counting one two three, one two three, laboured round with him at arm's length. 'Mrs. Ritchie, Jane's got a marvellous sense of rhythm.'

Roger danced on with Audrey. She looked very happy. Earlier in the day, Mrs. Carmichael had suggested that if you really looked, you saw that Audrey had fine eyes. Not untrue, perhaps? Enlarged, dark, they overcame her cheeks and softly glowed. She looked like a young girl.

Mrs. Ritchie took a turn round the room with John; but the syncopated insinuations of Reynaldo could not beguile John's ears or mollify his limbs, and they desisted amicably, by mutual consent.

'I can't teach you,' she said. 'I don't know how it's done. I can only follow. Perhaps if you watched Roger you could pick it up.'

'Oh, Roger,' he said, without scorn or bitterness; 'I could never pick up what *he's* got. Might as well tell me to pick up fencing by watching him. He's the best fencer the school's had for years.'

'Audrey's a good dancer too.'

'Mm.' He studied her feet as she passed. 'I suppose she is. I might get her to give me some tips.'

His mother shot a glance at him. Satirical? Not at all. Unaccountable youth. Or was it that despising her as he did in her person, her femininity, he could permit himself to make use of her accomplishments for his purposes; whereas Roger, unapproachable, hero-figure, must not even in imagination be exploited?

'Mrs. Ritchie, will you dance?'

She found herself gliding and turning easily in the circle of Roger's arm.

'Do you dance a lot?' she said after a while. 'But of course you do.'

'As much as I can. I had a marvellous party in London last week, and I hope to fit in another next week before I go home.'

'Are people really still dancing in London?'

'Oh, yes, rather. Like mad.' He sounded surprised. 'I suppose some parents do prefer to keep their daughters out of bombing range if possible, but there seem plenty left.'

'You dance beautifully,' she said. It was absurd: she could not refrain from feeling shy. I'm old enough to be his mother, she told herself. But it was his air of tolerant authority, his self-sufficiency, his elegance.

'Let me return the compliment.' He gave a little bow, a little laugh.

'I haven't danced for years,' she said.

'I adore it, I must say,' said Roger. 'My sister and I are going to give a little dance at home at the end of this month. It's her sixteenth birthday.'

'Have you a sister? That's nice. What is she like? Is she pretty?'

'Going to be, I think. She's a bit on and off still, but I think she'll make it.'

'Is she like you?'

'They say she's like me.' He gave another little laugh. He whirled with her, round and round, smoothly, at the end of the room. 'It's an odd thing,' he said as they started to glide on again, 'I *cannot* dance with my sister. I don't know why it is. My friends tell me she's quite a fair dancer, but so far as I'm concerned she might be a sack of potatoes.'

He sounded baffled, quite indignant. He was very young after all. She looked up at him and laughed. The tune came to an end. He kept his arm round her, waiting for the next one to begin. When it did, he said: 'Ah, my favourite waltz!' and started off with her again. It seemed strange to be dancing to tunes with which she was totally unfamiliar. She did not say so: it would make her part of what must be to him totally unfamiliar history. Mr. Carmichael had taken the floor with Audrey. An athletic waltzer of the old school, he dipped, swung, reversed her vigorously. Otherwise the sexes had become segregated. The little girls hopped about together, bunching each other's skirts up. The three boys circled together in the crouching attitude of a football scrum. From time to time Gerald broke out and did a few pirouettes and mincing runs with arms outstretched, on tiptoe. Presently Oliver tripped him up and they all fell together in a heap. The eyelids of Norman dropped lower, lower, closed entirely. Mrs. Ritchie said:

'I've put those cherry branches you gave us in a white vase in my bedroom. They look so beautiful. I can't tell you what pleasure they give me.'

'Good!' he said. 'They are nice.'

'Roger, I can never thank you properly for your playing to-night. You simply made the evening. You must have seen for yourself how much the village appreciated it. They'll never forget you.'

'I assure you,' he said, 'there's nothing to thank me for. I enjoyed myself hugely: it was pure self-indulgence. But it was a disgraceful noise, really it was. I'm hopelessly out of practice. I haven't touched the fiddle since I was at my private. I fancied myself as a Maestro then.' He uttered his characteristic amused two-note laugh.

'You're more interested in painting now?'

'Well… yes…' He considered. 'I suppose I am. I took to it about eighteen months ago. Mr. Carrington, that's the art master I expect you know, is responsible really. He encouraged me.'

'I saw two of your portraits in the drawing school when I went down to see John. I remember them very well. I was so impressed.'

'Did you really?' He sounded mildly surprised, mildly gratified. 'That's excellent news. I must say I find portraits fascinating.'

'You're going to go on with it? Make it your career?'

'I don't know. I do wonder.' He sounded impersonal, incurious. 'I'm in hot water all round at present. My Papa destines me for the family business. He doesn't care to see me idling about and fiddling with brushes. He's worried. Mr. Carrington's worried too. I appear to be stuck. My report says: Unable to finish anything. What is to be done?'

'It's just one of those bad patches. They're inevitable. You'll make a big step forward soon.' But she felt at a loss. What intuition, what secret principle was at work within him? What moved him? He was without ambition. Delightful dilettante, would he come to nothing?

'Jane's so excited about sitting for you,' she said. 'I'm afraid she may have a hang-over to-morrow and not look her best. You must be firm with her about sitting still. She'd do anything to please you – stand on her head if necessary.'

He laughed. 'She's a charming creature,' he said. 'I've quite lost my heart to her. She's incredibly paintable, isn't she?'

'Do you think so? I'm so glad.' She felt extreme gratification.

'Those gold lights in her skin. I really must paint her some day, if I may.'

After a pause, she said: 'Not to-morrow?'

'Well, actually I'm leaving to-morrow, I believe. I think I really must. Mr. and Mrs. Carmichael must have had enough of me.' He laughed. 'Besides I believe I'm expected elsewhere to-morrow.'

'What a pity.' A blow. A blow for Jane: better not break it to-night. 'Perhaps you'll be coming to stay again in the summer?'

'I do hope so,' he said. 'I've had such a perfect time. It's such incredibly beautiful country here.'

She said, feeling shy: 'Perhaps you'd come and stay with us some time. We'd all love it.'

'How very kind of you. That would be delightful. There's nothing I'd like better.' The tune died away. The voice of Reynaldo himself came on the air, crooned out a personal good-night. It was midnight. 'Unfortunately,' said Roger, 'the shades of the prison house will have closed on me by the summer. I shall be in the Army.'

'In the Army? As soon as that. I forgot. You're eighteen?'

'Eighteen last month.'

'Are you dreading it?'

'Oh, no.' He nodded. 'I'm rather looking forward to it.'

He would go into the Army, and be drilled and do fatigues and go on courses, and be sent to his O.C.T.U.[15] and get his commission, and have embarkation leave and vanish from England under security silence and... come to nothing?

'Perhaps the war will end,' she said.

She looked at him. He looked away over the room, smiling secretively. What was his meaning? 'You see, as things are, it's rather pointless really, isn't it, to commit myself, to choose, to have a future...' Was that it? Or had he no meaning?

Now this party was really over. The hostess's face looked tiny, mournful with weariness; the host yawned without restraint. That's what we shall remember most clearly about the war: everybody yawning, dropping with sleep. Jane submitted to her overcoat without demur. Her face was vacant. She was far past the point of asking Roger exactly what time to-morrow she was to be ready. Audrey came downstairs: during the last ten minutes she had removed the somnolent Norman and, like a good sister, stretched him in his bed. All the Carmichaels gathered at the front door with jokes, with thanks, with promises to telephone, with kisses and handshakes to speed their guests. Suddenly another note became added to the din: an urgent yodelling torn from a throat in the torments of dementia.

'*Puffles!*' cried Meg. 'Shut in my bedroom all this time. Oh, Puffles!'

Up she flew. Next moment down shot Puffles and hurled himself among them, gabbling, shrieking, swooning at their feet in circular swathes.

'Oh, Puffles, Puffles!' 'Oh, the poor man!' 'Shut in all the evening and never said a word!' 'Does he want to go outies then?' 'Mummy, we must take Puffles for a run to make up to him.' 'Good boy, outies, come on then.' 'Come on, let's all go. Mummy, we shan't be long. Just up the lane.'

The front door banged, shutting off Mr. and Mrs. Car-michael. Feet pounded down the darkness and away. Shouts, laughter diminished in the distance. Mrs. Ritchie grasped Jane to her side. They found themselves alone in the drive.

'Where've they gone?' said Jane, dazed, walking at her mother's side.

'Only just a little way up the lane with Puffles. You heard them say they'd be back very soon.'

'Did John go? And Audrey? Why couldn't I go? They went without telling me.'

'Oh, darling, it's nothing to miss. Just groping about in that pitch-dark muddy old lane. You wouldn't have enjoyed it a bit.'

'Did Meg go?'

'No, no, I'm sure Meg's going to bed this very moment.'

'I thought I saw her dash out of the door.'

'No.' Mrs. Ritchie suppressed an identical image.

'I'll ask her to-morrow. Did John ask you if he could go?'

'No, he didn't. He's a bad boy and I'm cross with him.'

'I wouldn't have thought Audrey would go without asking.'

The face of Audrey at the door came before Mrs. Ritchie; sparkling, eager, lost to decorum. 'I bet they won't come back for hours.'

Only too likely. She saw them ranging the countryside with whoop and chorus. I won't have it, she told herself, furious, impotent.

'Darling,' she said, 'I'm glad you stayed with me. I should have been sad going home alone.'

Jane pressed her hand. They crossed the lane and climbed the steep withy bank into the pasture, where open space made a faint lightening of the deep darkness.

'We forgot to bring a torch,' said Jane. 'Never mind. I like being out at night with you. Walking, walking, walking in

..re. It doesn't seem as if we were in the world at all.' She squeezed her hand tightly again.

'Oh, Jane, I haven't danced for years. Not since you were born.'

'Haven't you? You seemed to get on all right. I noticed you smiling. I'm so glad Roger didn't ask me to dance. I should have felt awful, not knowing how to.' She spoke with simple relief and satisfaction. 'Meg was telling me all about her school in New York while we were eating those ices. It was very interesting. She thinks their standard of education rather low in some ways. She was awfully behind in history when she came back. But up more in Current Events... Oh, Mummy, isn't Norman an awful boy? He took the very last piece of chocolate cake. He said: "Anybody want this? Then I will." Oh, he is awful.'

They reached the front door, opened it and went into their house. Mrs. Plumley had left one light burning in the sitting-room.

'I suppose I'd better leave it for those wicked creatures,' said Mrs. Ritchie. 'Quick to bed, darling.'

'Can't we wait up?' Jane rocked on her feet.

'No, no. I'm going to bed too. I shan't wait up.'

'Is it after midnight?'

'Long after.'

'Good!'

Half carrying Jane upstairs, Mrs. Ritchie pulled her clothes off, removed the remains of lipstick and rouge with face cream, brushed her hair cursorily.

'I can't be fished to do my teeth,' said Jane, falling into bed. 'Tell me the minute you hear them come in, won't you? I wonder if John likes Audrey any better now.'

They kissed. Mrs. Ritchie went down, took a sheet of paper, wrote on it in large print: 'Good-night. Go straight to bed'; left it propped against the lamp, went upstairs and undressed. Coming from the bathroom, she listened at Jane's half-open door. Deep breathing issued softly, rhythmically from the shadows.

She got into bed and lay with her bedside light on, staring at the tall white vase of cherry. Beautiful, beautiful, triumphant consolation. But one branch was withering already; and as she watched, a whole flurry of petals dropped down out of the sheaf and fell on the table.

Above the roof the arch of night began to throb through all its length and breadth: a strong force of our bombers passing overhead. She took up *Shakespeare's Images of Man and Nature* and read a few passages, but her eyelids dropped. She lay in a coma. It was just under an hour before she heard the front door creak open, close again. Cautious footsteps, whispers. They were trying to be quiet. She heard John's tread going through the kitchen to the larder, returning. He opened the cake tin noisily. They would be finishing off the dough cake. Another few minutes and Audrey came tiptoeing upstairs. 'Good-night,' called John from below: cheerful, friendly.

She leaned out towards the light to extinguish it. As she moved, something slipped out of the sheets on to the floor: Jane's writing pad. Of course, Jane had selected this bed to rest on and deal with her correspondence before the performance. She picked it up. She read:

Darling Angie, how are you? I shall be staying up till twelve o'clock to-night. We are having wonderful hol

Notes

1. Children's book by E. Nesbit, published in 1898.
2. Marie Louise Elisabeth Vigée-Lebrun, French neoclassical painter (1755–1842).
3. Nom de plume of poet Ruth Collie (1888–1936).
4. Historian, literary critic and translator Andrew Lang (1844–1912) collected and adapted numerous fairy tales.
5. Tragic character in Charles Dickens' *David Copperfield*.
6. Ham Peggotty's cousin and fiancé, another tragic figure in *David Copperfield*.
7. Writer and illustrator of children's books (1846–1901).
8. Welsh writer (1903–34). *Rhapsody* was published in 1927 to great acclaim.
9. Classic study of folklore, magic and religion, published from 1890–1915, by Sir James George Frazer (1854–1941).
10. French brand of glue with a distinctive smell.
11. Three fertility goddesses who had been deities of punishment under the name Erinyes (the Furies).
12. Painter (1878–1961).
13. Popular wartime radio programme. Its name was an abbreviation of the catchphrase 'It's That Man Again', used in newspapers whenever Hitler made a new territorial claim.
14. 'My God! You're not going to tell me, honestly, that that blasted boy is still there?... He is indeed, ready to jump out on us.'
'Let's kill him immediately.'
'No doubt it's because he's afraid.'
'You think? Poor little thing' (French).
15. Officer Cadet Training Unit.

Biographical note

Rosamond Lehmann was born in Buckinghamshire in 1901, the second daughter of Liberal MP and contributor to *Punch* R.C. Lehmann. Her brother, John Lehmann, was a poet, publisher and editor who was associated with the Bloomsbury group.

Lehmann was educated at Girton College, Cambridge, and married Leslie Runciman in 1922. It was an unhappy, childless marriage; they had separated by the time her first novel, *Dusty Answer*, was published in 1927. With its frank exploration of sexual desire it caused a sensation and made its author a modernist celebrity.

In 1928, Lehmann married the artist Wogan Philipps, with whom she had two children. In 1930 *A Note in Music* was published, which, like her first novel, created some degree of scandal. This and her next two novels, *Invitation to the Waltz* (1932) and its sequel *The Weather in the Streets* (1936), firmly established her reputation as a writer.

During the Second World War Lehmann contributed the five short stories in this edition to *New Writing*, her brother John's periodical, which were then published in 1946 as *The Gipsy's Baby*. *The Ballad and the Source* was published in 1944, followed by *The Echoing Grove* in 1953, which was made into a film, *The Heart of Me*, in 2002.

Lehmann published a short autobiographical work, *The Swan in the Evening: Fragments of an Inner Life*, in 1967, and *A Sea-Grape Tree*, a sequel to *The Ballad and the Source*, in 1976. She was created CBE in 1982, and died in 1990.

Author	Title	Foreword writer
Mikhail Bulgakov	*A Dog's Heart*	A.S. Byatt
Mikhail Bulgakov	*The Fatal Eggs*	Doris Lessing
Anthony Burgess	*The Eve of St Venus*	
Colette	*Claudine's House*	Doris Lessing
Marie Ferranti	*The Princess of Mantua*	
Beppe Fenoglio	*A Private Affair*	Paul Bailey
F. Scott Fitzgerald	*The Popular Girl*	Helen Dunmore
F. Scott Fitzgerald	*The Rich Boy*	John Updike
Graham Greene	*No Man's Land*	David Lodge
Franz Kafka	*Metamorphosis*	Martin Jarvis
Franz Kafka	*The Trial*	Zadie Smith
D.H. Lawrence	*Wintry Peacock*	Amit Chaudhuri
Carlo Levi	*Words are Stones*	Anita Desai
André Malraux	*The Way of the Kings*	Rachel Seiffert
Katherine Mansfield	*In a German Pension*	Linda Grant
Katherine Mansfield	*Prelude*	William Boyd
Vladimir Mayakovsky	*My Discovery of America*	Colum McCann
Luigi Pirandello	*Loveless Love*	
Françoise Sagan	*The Unmade Bed*	
Jean-Paul Sartre	*The Wall*	Justin Cartwright
Bernard Shaw	*The Adventures of the Black Girl in Her Search for God*	Colm Tóibín
Georges Simenon	*Three Crimes*	
Leonard Woolf	*A Tale Told by Moonlight*	Victoria Glendinning